N. E. Dalton.
Southwood Bookshop.
Highgate.
Nov. 1957

THE VOICE OF THE CITY

O. HENRY'S WORKS

PRICE 1/- EACH NET

THE VOICE OF THE CITY
ROLLING STONES
STRICTLY BUSINESS
THE GENTLE GRAFTER
OPTIONS
THE TRIMMED LAMP
SIXES AND SEVENS
HEART OF THE WEST
CABBAGES AND KINGS
THE FOUR MILLION
WHIRLIGIGS
ROADS OF DESTINY

THE O. HENRY BIOGRAPHY

By C. ALPHONSO SMITH

Illustrated.   Price 10/6 net

LONDON: HODDER AND STOUGHTON

THE VOICE
OF THE CITY

FURTHER STORIES OF
THE FOUR MILLION

By

O. HENRY

HODDER AND STOUGHTON
PUBLISHERS, LONDON
1916

CONTENTS

THE VOICE OF THE CITY

TWENTY-FIVE years ago the school children used to chant their lessons. The manner of their delivery was a singsong recitative between the utterance of an Episcopal minister and the drone of a tired sawmill. I mean no disrespect. We must have lumber and sawdust.

I remember one beautiful and instructive little lyric that emanated from the physiology class. The most striking line of it was this:

"The shin-bone is the long-est bone in the hu-man bod-y."

What an inestimable boon it would have been if all the corporeal and spiritual facts pertaining to man had thus been tunefully and logically inculcated in our youthful minds! But what we gained in anatomy, music and philosophy was meagre.

The other day I became confused. I needed a ray of light. I turned back to those school days for aid. But in all the nasal harmonies we whined forth from those hard benches I could not recall one that treated of the voice of agglomerated mankind.

In other words, of the composite vocal message of massed humanity.

In other words, of the Voice of a Big City.

Now, the individual voice is not lacking.

7

We can understand the song of the poet,
the ripple of the brook, the meaning of the
man who wants $5 until next Monday, the
inscriptions on the tombs of the Pharaohs,
the language of flowers, the " step lively " of
the conductor, and the prelude of the milk
cans at 4 A.M.   Certain large-eared ones even
assert that they are wise to the vibrations of
the tympanum produced by concussion of the
air emanating from Mr. H. James.   But who
can comprehend the meaning of the voice of
the city ?

I went out for to see.

First, I asked Aurelia.   She wore white
Swiss and a hat with flowers on it, and
ribbons and ends of things fluttered here and
there.

" Tell me," I said, stammeringly, for I have
no voice of my own, " what does this big—er—
enormous—er—whopping city say ?   It must
have a voice of some kind.   Does it ever
speak to you ?   How do you interpret its
meaning ?   It is a tremendous mass, but it
must have a key."

" Like a Saratoga trunk ? " asked Aurelia.

" No," said I.   " Please do not refer to the
lid.   I have a fancy that every city has a
voice.   Each one has something to say to the
one who can hear it.   What does the big one
say to you ? "

" All cities," said Aurelia, judicially, " say
the same thing.   When they get through

saying it there is an echo from Philadelphia
So, they are unanimous."

"Here are 4,000,000 people," said I,
scholastically, "compressed upon an island,
which is mostly lamb surrounded by Wall
Street water. The conjunction of so many
units into so small a space must result in an
identity—or, or rather a homogeneity—that
finds its oral expression through a common
channel. It is, as you might say, a consensus
of translation, concentrating in a crystallized,
general idea which reveals itself in what may
be termed the Voice of the City. Can you tell
me what it is ? "

Aurelia smiled wonderfully. She sat on the
high stoop. A spray of insolent ivy bobbed
against her right ear. A ray of impudent
moonlight flickered upon her nose. But I was
adamant, nickel-plated.

"I must go and find out," I said, "what
is the Voice of this city. Other cities have
voices. It is an assignment. I must have it.
New York," I continued, in a rising tone,
"had better not hand me a cigar and say :
'Old man, I can't talk for publication.' No
other city acts in that way. Chicago says,
unhesitatingly, 'I will ;' Philadelphia says,
'I should ;' New Orleans says, 'I used to ;'
Louisville says, 'Don't care if I do ;' St Louis
says, 'Excuse me ;' Pittsburg says, 'Smoke
up.' Now, New York —— "

Aurelia smiled.

"Very well," said I, "I must go elsewhere and find out."

I went into a palace, tile-floored, cherub-ceilinged, and square with the cop. I put my foot on the brass rail and said to Billy Magnus, the best bar-tender in the diocese :

"Billy, you've lived in New York a long time—what kind of a song-and-dance does this old town give you ? What I mean is, doesn't the gab of it seem to kind of bunch up and slide over the bar to you in a sort of amalgamated tip that hits off the burg in a kind of an epigram with a dash of bitters and a slice of —— "

"Excuse me a minute," said Billy, " somebody's punching the button at the side door."

He went away ; came back with an empty tin bucket ; again vanished with it full; returned and said to me :

"That was Mame. She rings twice. She likes a glass of beer for supper. Her and the kid. If you ever saw that little skeesicks of mine brace up in his high chair and take his beer and —— But, say, what was yours ? I get kind of excited when I hear them two rings—was it the baseball score or gin fizz you asked for ? "

"Ginger ale," I answered.

I walked up to Broadway. I saw a cop on the corner. The cops take kids up, women across, and men in. I went up to him.

"If I'm not exceeding the spiel limit,"

I said, " let me ask you. You see New York
during its vocative hours. It is the function
of you and your brother cops to preserve the
acoustics of the city. There must be a civic
voice that is intelligible to you. At night
during your lonely rounds you must have
heard it. What is the epitome of its turmoil
and shouting ? What does the city say to
you ? "

" Friend," said the policeman, spinning
his club, " it don't say nothing. I get my
orders from the man higher up. Say, I guess
you 're all right. Stand here for a few minutes
and keep an eye open for the roundsman."

The cop melted into the darkness of the
side street. In ten minutes he had returned.

" Married last Tuesday," he said, half
gruffly. " You know how they are. She
comes to that corner at nine every night for
a—comes to say ' hello ! ' I generally manage
to be there. Say, what was it you asked me
a bit ago—what 's doing in the city ? Oh,
there 's a roof-garden or two just opened,
twelve blocks up."

I crossed a crow's-foot of street-car tracks,
and skirted the edge of an umbrageous park.
An artificial Diana, gilded, heroic, poised,
wind-ruled, on the tower, shimmered in the
clear light of her namesake in the sky. Along
came my poet, hurrying, hatted, haired,
emitting dactyls, spondees and dactylis. I
seized him.

"Bill," said I (in the magazine he is Cleon), "give me a lift. I am on an assignment to find out the Voice of the city. You see, it's a special order. Ordinarily a symposium comprising the views of Henry Clews, John L. Sullivan, Edwin Markham, May Irwin and Charles Schwab would be about all. But this is a different matter. We want a broad, poetic, mystic vocalization of the city's soul and meaning. You are the very chap to give me a hint. Some years ago a man got at the Niagara Falls and gave us its pitch. The note was about two feet below the lowest G on the piano. Now, you can't put New York into a note unless it's better indorsed than that. But give me an idea of what it would say if it should speak. It is bound to be a mighty and far-reaching utterance. To arrive at it we must take the tremendous crash of the chords of the day's traffic, the laughter and music of the night, the solemn tones of Dr. Parkhurst, the rag-time, the weeping, the stealthy hum of cab-wheels, the shout of the press agent, the tinkle of fountains on the roof gardens, the hullabaloo of the strawberry vender and the covers of *Everybody's Magazine*, the whispers of the lovers in the parks—all these sounds must go into your Voice--not combined, but mixed, and of the mixture an essence made; and of the essence an extract —an audible extract, of which one drop shall form the thing we seek."

" Do you remember," asked the poet, with a chuckle, " that California girl we met at Stiver's studio last week ? Well, I 'm on my way to see her. She repeated that poem of mine, ' The Tribute of Spring,' word for word. She 's the smartest proposition in this town just at present. Say, how does this confounded tie look ? I spoiled four before I got one to set right."

" And the Voice that I asked you about ? " I inquired.

" Oh, she doesn't sing," said Cleon. " But you ought to hear her recite my ' Angel of the Inshore Wind.' "

I passed on. I cornered a newsboy, and he flashed at me prophetic pink papers that outstripped the news by two revolutions of the clock's longest hand.

" Son," I said, while pretended to chase coins in my penny pocket, " doesn't it sometimes seem to you as if the city ought to be able to talk ? All these ups and downs and funny business and queer things happening every day—what would it say, do you think, if it could speak ? "

" Quit yer kiddin'," said the boy. " Wot paper yer want ? I got no time to waste. It 's Mag's birthday, and I want thirty cents to git her a present."

Here was no interpreter of the city's mouthpiece. I bought a paper, and consigned its undeclared treaties, its premeditated

murders and unfought battles to an ash
can.

Again I repaired to the park and sat in the
moon shade. I thought and thought, and
wondered why none could tell me what I asked
for.

And then, as swift as light from a fixed star,
the answer came to me. I arose and hurried
—hurried as so many reasoners must, back
around my circle. I knew the answer, and I
hugged it in my breast as I flew, fearing lest
someone would stop me and demand my
secret.

Aurelia was still on the stoop. The moon
was higher and the ivy shadows were deeper.
I sat at her side, and we watched a little cloud
tilt at the drifting moon and go asunder, quite
pale and discomfited.

And then, wonder of wonders and delight of
delights! our hands somehow touched, and our
fingers closed together and did not part.

After half an hour Aurelia said, with that
smile of hers :

" Do you know, you haven't spoken a word
since you came back ! "

"That," said I, nodding wisely, " is the
Voice of the City."

THE COMPLETE LIFE OF
JOHN HOPKINS

THERE is a saying that no man has tasted the
full flavour of life until he has known poverty,
love, and war. The justness of this reflection
commends it to the lover of condensed
philosophy. The three conditions embrace
about all there is in life worth knowing. A
surface thinker might deem that wealth should
be added to the list. Not so. When a poor
man finds a long-hidden quarter-dollar that
has slipped through a rip into his vest lining,
he sounds the pleasure of life with a deeper
plummet than any millionaire can hope to
cast.

It seems that the wise executive power that
rules life has thought best to drill man in these
three conditions; and none may escape all
three. In rural places the terms do not mean
so much. Poverty is less pinching; love is
temperate; war shrinks to contests about
boundary-lines and the neighbours' hens. It
is in the cities that our epigram gains in truth
and vigour; and it has remained for one
John Hopkins to crowd the experience into a
rather small space of time.

The Hopkins flat was like a thousand others.
There was a rubber plant in one window; a

flea-bitten terrier sat in the other, wondering when he was to have his day.

John Hopkins was like a thousand others. He worked at $20 per week in a nine-story, red-brick building at either Insurance, Buckle's Hoisting Engines, Chiropody, Loans, Pulleys, Boas Renovated, Waltz Guaranteed in Five Lessons, or Artificial Limbs. It is not for us to wring Mr. Hopkins's avocation from these outward signs that be.

Mrs. Hopkins was like a thousand others. The auriferous tooth, the sedentary disposition, the Sunday afternoon wanderlust, the draught upon the delicatessen store for home-made comforts, the furor for department store marked-down sales, the feeling of superiority to the lady in the third-floor front who wore genuine ostrich tips and had two names over her bell, the mucilaginous hours during which she remained glued to the window-sill, the vigilant avoidance of the instalment man, the tireless patronage of the acoustics of the dumb-waiter shaft—all the attributes of the Gotham flat-dweller were hers.

One moment yet of sententiousness and the story moves.

In the Big City large and sudden things happen. You round a corner and thrust the rib of your umbrella into the eye of your old friend from Kootenai Falls. You stroll out to pluck a Sweet William in the park—and lo ! bandits attack you—you are ambulanced to the hospital—you marry your nurse; are divorced—get squeezed while short on U. P. S. and D. O. W. N. S.—stand in the bread line— marry an heiress, take out your laundry and pay your club dues—seemingly all in the wink of an eye. You travel the streets, and a finger beckons to you, a handkerchief is dropped for you, a brick is dropped upon you, the elevator cable or your bank breaks, a table d'hôte or your wife disagrees with you, and Fate tosses you about like cork crumbs in wine opened by an un-feed waiter. The City is a sprightly youngster, and you are red paint upon its toy, and you get licked off.

John Hopkins sat, after a compressed dinner, in his glove-fitting, straight-front flat. He sat upon a hornblende couch and gazed, with satiated eyes, at Art Brought Home to the People in the shape of " The Storm " tacked against the wall. Mrs. Hopkins discoursed droningly of the dinner smells from the flat across the hall. The flea-bitten terrier gave Hopkins a look of disgust, and showed a man-hating tooth.

Here was neither poverty, love, nor war; but upon such barren stems may be grafted those essentials of a complete life.

John Hopkins sought to inject a few raisins of conversation into the tasteless dough of existence. " Putting a new elevator in at the office," he said, discarding the nominative noun, " and the boss has turned out his whiskers."

"You don't mean it!" commented Mrs. Hopkins.

"Mr Whipples," continued John, "wore his new spring suit down to-day. I liked it fine. It's a grey with —— " He stopped, suddenly stricken by a need that made itself known to him. "I believe I 'll walk down to the corner and get a five-cent cigar," he concluded.

John Hopkins took his hat and picked his way down the musty halls and stairs of the flat-house.

The evening air was mild, and the streets shrill with the careless cries of children playing games controlled by mysterious rhythms and phrases. Their elders held the doorways and steps with leisurely pipe and gossip. Paradoxically, the fire-escapes supported lovers in couples, who made no attempt to fly the mounting conflagration they were there to fan.

The corner cigar store aimed at by John Hopkins was kept by a man named Freshmayer, who looked upon the earth as a sterile promontory.

Hopkins, unknown in the store, entered and called genially for his "bunch of spinach, car-fare grade." This imputation deepened the pessimism of Freshmayer; but he set out a brand that came perilously near to filling the order. Hopkins bit off the roots of his purchase, and lighted up at the swinging gas-jet. Feeling in his pockets to make payment, he found not a penny there.

"Say, my friend," he explained, frankly, "I've come out without any change. Hand you that nickel first time I pass."

Joy surged in Freshmayer's heart. Here was corroboration of his belief that the world was rotten and man a peripatetic evil. Without a word he rounded the end of his counter and made earnest onslaught upon his customer. Hopkins was no man to serve as a punching-bag for a pessimistic tobacconist. He quickly bestowed upon Freshmayer a colorado-maduro eye in return for the ardent kick that he received from that dealer in goods for cash only.

The impetus of the enemy's attack forced the Hopkins line back to the sidewalk. There the conflict raged ; the pacific wooden Indian, with his carven smile, was overturned, and those of the street who delighted in carnage pressed round to view the zealous joust.

But then came the inevitable cop and imminent inconvenience for both the attacker and attacked. John Hopkins was a peaceful citizen, who worked at rebuses of nights in a flat, but he was not without the fundamental spirit of resistance that comes with the battle-rage. He knocked the policeman into a grocer's sidewalk display of goods, and gave Freshmayer a punch that caused him temporarily to regret that he had not made it a rule to extend a five-cent line of credit to certain customers.

Then Hopkins took spiritedly to his heels down the sidewalk, closely followed by the cigar-dealer and the policeman, whose uniform testified to the reason in the grocer's sign that read : " Eggs cheaper than anywhere else in the city."

As Hopkins ran he became aware of a big, low, red, racing automobile that kept abreast of him in the street. This auto steered in to the side of the sidewalk, and the man guiding it motioned to Hopkins to jump into it. He did so without slackening his speed, and fell into the turkey-red upholstered seat beside the chauffeur. The big machine, with a diminuendo cough, flew away like an albatross down the avenue into which the street emptied.

The driver of the auto sped his machine without a word. He was masked beyond guess in the goggles and diabolic garb of the chauffeur.

" Much obliged, old man," called Hopkins, gratefully. " I guess you 've got sporting blood in you, all right, and don't admire the sight of two men trying to soak one. Little more and I 'd have been pinched."

The chauffeur made no sign that he had heard. Hopkins shrugged a shoulder and chewed at his cigar, to which his teeth had clung grimly throughout the mêlée.

Ten minutes and the auto turned into the open carriage entrance of a noble mansion of brown stone, and stood still. The chauffeur leaped out, and said :

"Come quick. The lady, she will explain. It is the great honour you will have, monsieur. Ah, that milady could call upon Armand to do this thing! But, no, I am only one chauffeur."

With vehement gestures the chauffeur conducted Hopkins into the house. He was ushered into a small but luxurious reception chamber. A lady, young, and possessing the beauty of visions, rose from a chair. In her eyes smouldered a becoming anger. Her high-arched, thread-like brows were ruffled into a delicious frown.

"Milady," said the chauffeur, bowing low, "I have the honour to relate to you that I went to the house of Monsieur Long and found him to be not at home. As I came back I see this gentleman in combat against—how you say—greatest odds. He is fighting with five—ten—thirty men—gendarmes, *aussi*. Yes, milady, he what you call 'swat' one—three—eight policemans. If that Monsieur Long is out, I say to myself this gentleman he will serve milady so well, and I bring him here."

"Very well, Armand," said the lady, "you may go." She turned to Hopkins.

"I sent my chauffeur," she said, "to bring my cousin, Walter Long. There is a man in this house who has treated me with insult and abuse. I have complained to my aunt, and she laughs at me. Armand says you are brave. In these prosaic days men who are both brave and chivalrous are few. May I count upon your assistance ? "

John Hopkins thrust the remains of his cigar into his coat pocket. He looked upon this winning creature and felt his first thrill of romance. It was a knightly love, and contained no disloyalty to the flat with the flea-bitten terrier and the lady of his choice. He had married her after a picnic of the Lady Label Stickers' Union, Lodge No. 2, on a dare and a bet of new hats and chowder all around with his friend Billy McManus. This angel who was begging him to come to her rescue was something too heavenly for chowder, ·and as for hats—golden, jewelled crowns for her !

" Say," said John Hopkins, " just show me the guy that you 've got the grouch at. I 've neglected my talents as a scrapper heretofore, but this is my busy night."

" He is in there," said the lady, pointing to a closed door. " Come. Are you sure that you do not falter or fear ? "

" Me ? " said John Hopkins. " Just give me one of those roses in the bunch you are wearing, will you ? "

The lady gave him a red, red rose. John Hopkins kissed it, stuffed it into his vest pocket, opened the door, and walked into the room. It was a handsome library, softly but brightly lighted. A young man was there, reading.

" Books on etiquette is what you want to

study," said John Hopkins, abruptly. " Get up here, and I 'll give you some lessons. Be rude to a lady, will you ? "

The young man looked mildly surprised. Then he arose languidly, dexterously caught the arms of John Hopkins, and conducted him irresistibly to the front door of the house.

" Beware, Ralph Branscombe," cried the lady, who had followed, " what you do to the gallant man who has tried to protect me."

The young man shoved John Hopkins gently out the door and then closed it.

" Bess," he said calmly, " I wish you would quit reading historical novels. How in the world did that fellow get in here ? "

" Armand brought him," said the young lady. " I think you are awfully mean not to let me have that St. Bernard. I sent Armand for Walter. I was so angry with you."

" Be sensible, Bess," said the young man, taking her arm. " That dog isn't safe. He has bitten two or three people around the kennels. Come now, let 's go and tell auntie we are in good humour again."

Arm in arm, they moved away.

John Hopkins walked to his flat. The janitor's five-year-old daughter was playing on the steps. Hopkins gave her a nice red rose and walked upstairs.

Mrs. Hopkins was philandering with curl-papers.

" Get your cigar ? " she asked, disinterestedly.

"Sure," said Hopkins, "and I knocked around a while outside. It's a nice night."

He sat upon the hornblende sofa, took out the stump of his cigar, lighted it, and gazed at the graceful figures in "The Storm" on the opposite wall.

"I was telling you," said he, "about Mr. Whipples's suit. It's a grey, with an invisible check, and it looks fine."

A LICKPENNY LOVER

THERE were 3,000 girls in the Biggest Store. Masie was one of them. She was eighteen, and a saleslady in the gents' gloves. Here she became versed in two varieties of human beings—the kind of gents who buy their gloves in department stores and the kind of women who buy gloves for unfortunate gents. Besides this wide knowledge of the human species, Masie had acquired other information. She had listened to the promulgated wisdom of the 2,999 other girls, and had stored it in a brain that was as secretive and wary as that of a Maltese cat. Perhaps Nature, foreseeing that she would lack wise counsellors, had mingled the saving ingredient of shrewdness along with her beauty, as she has endowed the silver fox of the priceless fur above the other animals with cunning.

For Masie was beautiful. She was a deep-tinted blonde, with the calm poise of a lady who cooks butter cakes in a window. She stood behind her counter in the Biggest Store ; and as you closed your hand over the tape-line for your glove measure you thought of Hebe ; and as you looked again you wondered how she had come by Minerva's eyes.

When the floor-walker was not looking Masie

chewed tutti frutti ; when he was looking she
gazed up as if at the clouds and smiled
wistfully.

That is the shopgirl smile, and I enjoin you to
shun it unless you are well fortified with callosity
of the heart, caramels, and a congeniality for
the capers of Cupid. This smile belonged to
Masie's recreation hours and not to the store ;
but the floor-walker must have his own. He is
the Shylock of the stores. When he comes
nosing around the bridge of his nose is a toll-
bridge. It is goo-goo eyes or " git " when
he looks toward a pretty girl. Of course, not
all floor-walkers are thus. Only a few days
ago the papers printed news of one over eighty
years of age.

On day Irving Carter, painter, millionaire,
traveller, poet, automobilist, happened to
enter the Biggest Store. It is due to him to
add that his visit was not voluntary. Filial
duty took him by the collar and dragged him
inside, while his mother philandered among
the bronze and terra-cotta statuettes.

Carter strolled across to the glove counter
in order to shoot a few minutes on the wing.
His need for gloves was genuine ; he had
forgotten to bring a pair with him. But his
action hardly calls for apology, because he
had never heard of glove-counter flirtations.

As he neared the vicinity of his fate he
hesitated, suddenly conscious of this unknown
phase of Cupid's less worthy profession

Three or four cheap fellows, sonorously garbed, were leaning over the counters, wrestling with the mediatorial hand-coverings, while giggling girls played vivacious seconds to their lead upon the strident string of coquetry. Carter would have retreated, but he had gone too far. Masie confronted him behind her counter with a questioning look in eyes as coldly, beautifully, warmly blue as the glint of summer sunshine on an iceberg drifting in southern seas.

And then Irving Carter, painter, millionaire, etc., felt a warm flush rise to his aristocratically pale face. But not from diffidence. The blush was intellectual in origin. He knew in a moment that he stood in the ranks of the ready-made youths who wooed the giggling girls at other counters. Himself leaned against the oaken trysting-place of a cockney Cupid with a desire in his heart for the favour of a glove salesgirl. He was no more than Bill and Jack and Mickey. And then he felt a sudden tolerance for them, and an elating, courageous contempt for the conventions upon which he had fed, and an unhesitating determination to have this perfect creature for his own.

When the gloves were paid for and wrapped Carter lingered for a moment. The dimples at the corners of Masie's damask mouth deepened. All gentlemen who bought gloves lingered in just that way. She curved an arm, showing like Psyche's through her

shirt-waist sleeve, and rested an elbow upon
the show-case edge.

Carter had never before encountered a
situation of which he had not been perfect
master. But now he stood far more awkward
than Bill or Jack or Mickey. He had no chance
of meeting this beautiful girl socially. His
mind struggled to recall the nature and habits
of shopgirls as he had read or heard of them.
Somehow he had received the idea that they
sometimes did not insist too strictly upon the
regular channels of introduction. His heart
beat loudly at the thought of proposing an
unconventional meeting with this lovely and
virginal being. But the tumult in his heart
gave him courage.

After a few friendly and well-received remarks
on general subjects, he laid his card by her hand
on the counter.

" Will you please pardon me," he said,
" if I seem too bold ; but I earnestly hope
you will allow me the pleasure of seeing
you again. There is my name ; I assure
you that it is with the greatest respect that
I ask the favour of becoming one of your
fr—acquaintances. May I not hope for the
privilege ? "

Masie knew men—especially men who buy
gloves. Without hesitation she looked him
frankly and smilingly in the eyes, and said :

" Sure. I guess you 're all right. I don't
usually go out with strange gentlemen, though.

It ain't quite ladylike. When should you want to see me again ? "

" As soon as I may," said Carter. " If you would allow me to call at your home, I —— "

Masie laughed musically. " Oh, gee, no ! " she said, emphatically. " If you could see our flat once ! There's five of us in three rooms. I'd just like to see ma's face if I was to bring a gentleman friend there ! "

" Anywhere, then," said the enamoured Carter, " that will be convenient to you."

" Say," suggested Masie, with a bright-idea look in her peach-blow face, " I guess Thursday night will about suit me. Suppose you come to the corner of Eighth Avenue and Forty-eighth Street at 7.30. I live right near the corner. But I've got to be back home by eleven. Ma never lets me stay out after eleven."

Carter promised gratefully to keep the tryst, and then hastened to his mother, who was looking about for him to ratify her purchase of a bronze Diana.

A salesgirl, with small eyes and an obtuse nose, strolled near Masie, with a friendly leer.

" Did you make a hit with his nobs, Masie ? " she asked, familiarly.

" The gentleman asked permission to call," answered Masie, with the grand air as she slipped Carter's card into the bosom of her waist.

" Permission to call ! " echoed small eyes, with a snigger. " Did he say anything about dinner in the Waldorf and a spin in his auto afterward ? "

" Oh, cheese it ! " said Masie, wearily. " You 've been used to swell things, I don't think. You 've had a swelled head ever since that hose-cart driver took you out to a chop suey joint. No, he never mentioned the Waldorf ; but there 's a Fifth Avenue address on his card, and if he buys the supper you can bet your life there won't be no pigtail on the waiter what takes the order."

As Carter glided away from the Biggest Store with his mother in his electric runabout, he bit his lip with a dull pain at his heart. He knew that love had come to him for the first time in all the twenty-nine years of his life. And that the object of it should make so readily an appointment with him at a street corner, though it was a step toward his desires, tortured him with misgivings.

Carter did not know the shopgirl. He did not know that her home is often either a scarcely habitable tiny room or a domicile filled to overflowing with kith and kin. The street-corner is her parlour, the park is her drawing-room, the avenue is her garden walk ; yet for the most part she is as inviolate mistress of herself in them as is my lady inside her tapestried chamber.

One evening at dusk, two weeks after their first meeting, Carter and Masie strolled arm-in-arm into a little, dimly-lit park. They found a bench, tree-shadowed and secluded, and sat there.

For the first time his arm stole gently around her. Her golden-bronze head slid restfully against his shoulder.

" Gee ! " sighed Masie, thankfully. " Why didn't you ever think of that before ? "

" Masie," said Carter, earnestly, " you surely know that I love you. I ask you sincerely to marry me. You know me well enough by this time to have no doubts of me. I want you, and I must have you. I care nothing for the difference in our stations."

" What is the difference ? " asked Masie, curiously.

" Well, there isn't any," said Carter, quickly, " except in the minds of foolish people. It is in my power to give you a life of luxury. My social position is beyond dispute, and my means are ample."

" They all say that," remarked Masie. " It 's the kid they all give you. I suppose you really work in a delicatessen or follow the races. I ain't as green as I look."

" I can furnish you all the proofs you want," said Carter, gently. " And I want you, Masie. I loved you the first day I saw you."

" They all do," said Masie, with an amused laugh, " to hear 'em talk. If I could meet a man that got stuck on me the third time he 'd seen me I think I 'd get mashed on him."

" Please don't say such things," pleaded

Carter. " Listen to me, dear. Ever since I
first looked into your eyes you have been the
only woman in the world for me."

" Oh, ain't you the kidder ! " smiled Masie.
" How many other girls did you ever tell
that ? "

But Carter persisted. And at length he
reached the flimsy, fluttering little soul of the
shopgirl that existed somewhere deep down in
her lovely bosom. His words penetrated the
heart whose very lightness was its safest armour.
She looked up at him with eyes that saw.
And a warm glow visited her cool cheeks.
Tremblingly, awfully, her moth wings closed,
and she seemed about to settle upon the flower
of love. Some faint glimmer of life and its
possibilities on the other side of her glove
counter dawned upon her. Carter felt the
change and crowded the opportunity.

" Marry me, Masie," he whispered softly,
" and we will go away from this ugly city to
beautiful ones. We will forget work and
business, and life will be one long holiday. I
know where I should take you—I have been
there often. Just think of a shore where
summer is eternal, where the waves are always
rippling on the lovely beach and the people
are happy and free as children. We will sail
to those shores and remain there as long as
you please. In one of those far-away cities
there are grand and lovely palaces and towers
'ull of beautiful pictures and statues. The

streets of the city are water, and one travels about in —— "

" I know," said Masie, sitting up suddenly. " Gondolas."

" Yes," smiled Carter.

" I thought so," said Masie.

" And then," continued Carter, " we will travel on and see whatever we wish in the world. After the European cities we will visit India and the ancient cities there, and ride on elephants and see the wonderful temples of the Hindoos and Brahmins, and the Japanese gardens, and the camel trains and chariot races in Persia, and all the queer sights of foreign countries. Don't you think you would like it, Masie ? "

Masie rose to her feet.

" I think we had better be going home," she said, coolly. " It 's getting late."

Carter humoured her. He had come to know her varying, thistle-down moods, and that it was useless to combat them. But he felt a certain happy triumph. He had held for a moment, though but by a silken thread, the soul of his wild Psyche, and hope was stronger within him. Once she had folded her wings and her cool hand had closed about his own.

At the Biggest Store the next day Masie's chum, Lulu, waylaid her in an angle of the counter.

" How are you and your swell friend making it ? " she asked.

"Oh, him?" said Masie, patting her side curls. "He ain't in it any more. Say, Lu, what do you think that fellow wanted me to do?"

"Go on the stage?" guessed Lulu, breathlessly.

"Nit; he's too cheap a guy for that. He wanted me to marry him and go down to Coney Island for a wedding tour!"

DOUGHERTY'S EYE-OPENER

BIG JIM DOUGHERTY was a sport. He belonged to that race of men. In Manhattan it is a distinct race. They are the Caribs of the North —strong, artful, self-sufficient, clannish, honourable within the laws of their race, holding in lenient contempt neighbouring tribes who bow to the measure of Society's tape-line. I refer, of course, to the titled nobility of sportdom. There is a class which bears as a qualifying adjective the substantive belonging to a wind instrument made of a cheap and base metal. But the tin mines of Cornwall never produced the material for manufacturing descriptive nomenclature for " Big Jim " Dougherty.

The habitat of the sport is the lobby or the outside corner of certain hotels and combination restaurants and cafés. They are mostly men of different sizes, running from small to large ; but they are unanimous in the possession of a recently - shaven, blue-black cheek and chin and dark overcoats (in season) with black velvet collars.

Of the domestic life of the sport little is known It has been said that Cupid and Hymen sometimes take a hand in the game and copper the queen of hearts to lose. Daring theorists have averred—not content with simply saying—that a sport often contracts a spouse, and even incurs descendants. Sometimes he sits in the game of politics ; and then at chowder picnics there is a revelation of a Mrs. Sport and little Sports in glazed hats with tin pails.

But mostly the sport is Oriental.   He believes his women-folk should not be too patent. Somewhere behind grilles or flower-ornamented fire-escapes they await him.   There, no doubt, they tread on rugs from Teheran and are diverted by the bulbul and play upon the dulcimer and feed upon sweetmeats.   But away from his home the sport is an integer.   He does not, as men of other races in Manhattan do, become the convoy in his unoccupied hours of fluttering laces and high heels that tick off delectably the happy seconds of the evening parade.   He herds with his own race at corners, and delivers a commentary in his Carib lingo upon the passing show.

" Big Jim " Dougherty had a wife, but he did not wear a button portrait of her upon his lapel.   He had a home in one of those brownstone, iron-railed streets on the west side that look like a recently-excavated bowling alley of Pompeii.

To this home of his Mr. Dougherty repaired each night when the hour was so late as to promise no further diversion in the arch domains of sport.   By that time the occupant

of the monogamistic harem would be in dream-
land, the bulbul silenced, and the hour propitious
for slumber.

" Big Jim " always arose at twelve, meridian,
for breakfast, and soon afterward he would
return to the rendezvous of his " crowd."

He was always vaguely conscious that there
was a Mrs. Dougherty. He would have received
without denial the charge that the quiet, neat,
comfortable little woman across the table at
home was his wife. In fact, he remembered
pretty well that they had been married for
nearly four years. She would often tell him
about the cute tricks of Spot, the canary, and
the light-haired lady that lived in the window
of the flat across the street.

" Big Jim " Dougherty even listened to this
conversation of hers sometimes. He knew
that she would have a nice dinner ready for
him every evening at seven when he came for
it. She sometimes went to matinées, and she
had a talking machine with six dozen records.
Once when her Uncle Amos blew in on a wind
from up-state, she went with him to the Eden
Musée. Surely these things were diversions
enough for any woman.

One afternoon Mr. Dougherty finished his
breakfast, put on his hat, and got away fairly
for the door. When his hand was on the knob
he heard his wife's voice.

" Jim," she said, firmly, " I wish you would
take me out to dinner this evening. It has

2 *

been three years since you have been outside
the door with me."

" Big Jim " was astounded. She had never
asked anything like this before. It had the
flavour of a totally new proposition. But he
was a game sport.

" All right," he said. " You be ready when
I come at seven. None of this ' wait two
minutes till I primp an hour or two ' kind of
business, now, Dele."

" I 'll be ready," said his wife, calmly.

At seven she descended the stone steps in
the Pompeian bowling alley at the side of
" Big Jim " Dougherty. She wore a dinner
gown made of a stuff that the spiders must
have woven, and of a colour that a twilight
sky must have contributed. A light coat with
many admirably unnecessary capes and
adorably inutile ribbons floated downward
from her shoulders. Fine feathers do make
fine birds ; and the only reproach in the saying
is for the man who refuses to give up his earnings
to the ostrich-tip industry.

" Big Jim " Dougherty was troubled. There
was a being at his side whom he did not know.
He thought of the sober-hued plumage that this
bird of paradise was accustomed to wear in
her cage, and this winged revelation puzzled
him. In some way she reminded him of the
Delia Cullen that he had married four years
before. Shyly and rather awkwardly he
stalked at her right hand.

"After dinner I'll take you back home, Dele," said Mr. Dougherty, "and then I'll drop back up to Seltzer's with the boys. You can have swell chuck to-night if you want it. I made a winning on Anaconda yesterday; so you can go as far as you like."

Mr. Dougherty had intended to make the outing with his unwonted wife an inconspicuous one. Uxoriousness was a weakness that the precepts of the Caribs did not countenance. If any of his friends of the track, the billiard cloth or the square circle had wives they had never complained of the fact in public. There were a number of table d'hôte places on the cross streets near the broad and shining way; and to one of these he had purposed to escort her, so that the bushel might not be removed from the light of his domesticity.

But while on the way Mr. Dougherty altered those intentions. He had been casting stealthy glances at his attractive companion, and he was seized with the conviction that she was no selling-plater. He resolved to parade with his wife past Seltzer's café, where at this time a number of his tribe would be gathered to view the daily evening procession. Yes; and he would take her to dine at Hoogley's, the swellest slow-lunch warehouse on the line, he said to himself.

The congregation of smooth-faced tribal gentlemen were on watch at Seltzer's. As Mr. Dougherty and his reorganized Delia passed they stared, momentarily petrified, and then removed their hats—a performance as unusual to them as was the astonishing innovation presented to their gaze by " Big Jim." On the latter gentleman's impassive face there appeared a slight flicker of triumph—a faint flicker, no more to be observed than the expression called there by the draft of little casino to a four-card spade flush.

Hoogley's was animated. Electric lights shone—as, indeed, they were expected to do. And the napery, the glassware and the flowers also meritoriously performed the spectacular duties required of them. The guests were numerous, well-dressed and gay.

A waiter—not necessarily obsequious—conducted " Big Jim " Dougherty and his wife to a table.

" Play that menu straight across for what you like, Dele," said " Big Jim." " It 's you for a trough of the gilded oats to-night. It strikes me that maybe we 've been sticking too fast to home fodder."

" Big Jim's " wife gave her order. He looked at her with respect. She had mentioned truffles ; and he had not known that she knew what truffles were. From the wine list she designated an appropriate and desirable brand. He looked at her with some admiration.

She was beaming with the innocent excitement that woman derives from the exercise of her gregariousness. She was talking to

him about a hundred things with animation
and delight. And as the meal progressed her
cheeks, colourless from a life indoors, took
on a delicate flush. " Big Jim " looked around
the room and saw that none of the women there
had her charm. And then he thought of the
three years she had suffered immurement,
uncomplaining, and a flush of shame warmed
him, for he carried fair play as an item in his
creed.

But when the Honourable Patrick Corrigan,
leader in Dougherty's district and a friend of
his, saw them and came over to the table,
matters got to the three-quarter stretch. The
Honourable Patrick was a gallant man, both
in deeds and words. As for the Blarney Stone,
his previous actions toward it must have been
pronounced. Heavy damages for breach of
promise could surely have been obtained
had the Blarney Stone seen fit to sue the
Honourable Patrick.

" Jimmy, old man ! " he called ; he clapped
Dougherty on the back ; he shone like a midday
sun upon Delia.

"Honourable Mr. Corrigan—Mrs. Dougherty,"
said " Big Jim."

The Honourable Patrick became a fountain of
entertainment and admiration. The waiter
had to fetch a third chair for him ; he made
another at the table, and the wineglasses were
refilled.

" You selfish old rascal ! " he exclaimed,

shaking an arch finger at " Big Jim," " to have kept Mrs. Dougherty a secret from us."

And then " Big Jim " Dougherty, who was no talker, sat dumb, and saw the wife who had dined every evening for three years at home, blossom like a fairy flower. Quick, witty, charming, full of light and ready talk, she received the experienced attack of the Honourable Patrick on the field of repartee and surprised, vanquished, delighted him. She unfolded her long-closed petals, and around her the room became a garden. They tried to include " Big Jim " in the conversation, but he was without a vocabulary.

And then a stray bunch of politicians and good fellows who lived for sport came into the room. They saw " Big Jim " and the leader, and over they came and were made acquainted with Mrs. Dougherty. And in a few minutes she was holding a salon. Half a dozen men surrounded her, courtiers all, and six found her capable of charming. " Big Jim " sat, grim, and kept saying to himself : " Three years, three years ! "

The dinner came to an end. The Honourable Patrick reached for Mrs. Dougherty's cloak ; but that was a matter of action instead of words, and Dougherty's big hand got it first by two seconds.

While the farewells were being said at the door the Honourable Patrick smote Dougherty mightily between the shoulders.

" Jimmy, me boy," he declared, in a giant

whisper, "the madam is a jewel of the first water." Ye 're a lucky dog."

"Big Jim" walked homeward with his wife. She seemed quite as pleased with the lights and show windows in the streets as with the admiration of the men in Hoogley's. As they passed Seltzer's they heard the sound of many voices in the café. The boys would be starting the drinks around now and discussing past performances.

At the door of their home Delia paused. The pleasure of the outing radiated softly from her countenance. She could not hope for Jim of evenings, but the glory of this one would lighten her lonely hours for a long time.

"Thank you for taking me out, Jim," she said, gratefully. "You 'll be going back up to Seltzer's now, of course."

"To —— with Seltzer's," said "Big Jim," emphatically. "And d—— Pat Corrigan! Does he think I haven't got any eyes?"

And the door closed behind both of them.

"LITTLE SPECK IN GARNERED FRUIT"

THE honeymoon was at its full. There was a flat with the reddest of new carpets, tasselled portières and six steins with pewter lids arranged on a ledge above the wainscoting of the dining-room. The wonder of it was yet upon them. Neither of them had ever seen a yellow primrose by the river's brim ; but if such a sight had met their eyes at that time it would have seemed like—well, whatever the poet expected the right kind of people to see in it besides a primrose.

The bride sat in the rocker with her feet resting upon the world. She was wrapt in rosy dreams and a kimono of the same hue. She wondered what the people in Greenland and Tasmania and Beloochistan were saying one to another about her marriage to Kid McGarry. Not that it made any difference. There was no welter-weight from London to the Southern Cross that could stand up four hours—no ; four rounds—with her bridegroom. And he had been hers for three weeks ; and the crook of her little finger could sway him more than the fist of any 142-pounder in the world.

Love, when it is ours, is the other name

for self-abnegation and sacrifice. When it belongs to people across the airshaft it means arrogance and self-conceit.

The bride crossed her Oxfords and looked thoughtfully at the distemper Cupids on the ceiling.

" Precious," said she, with the air of Cleopatra asking Antony for Rome done up in tissue paper and delivered at residence, " I think I would like a peach."

Kid McGarry arose and put on his coat and hat. He was serious, shaven. sentimental, and spry.

" All right," said he, as coolly as though he were only agreeing to sign articles to fight the champion of England. " I 'll step down and cop one out for you—see ? "

" Don't be long," said the bride. " I 'll be lonesome without my naughty boy. Get a nice, ripe one."

After a series of farewells that would have befitted an imminent voyage to foreign parts, the Kid went down to the street.

Here he not unreasonably hesitated, for the season was yet early spring, and there seemed small chance of wresting anywhere from those chill streets and stores the coveted luscious guerdon of summer's golden prime.

At the Italian's fruit-stand on the corner he stopped and cast a contemptuous eye over the display of papered oranges, highly polished apples and wan, sun-hungry bananas.

"Gotta da peach?" asked the Kid in the tongue of Dante, the lover of lovers.

"Ah, no," sighed the vender. "Not for one mont com-a da peach. Too soon. Gotta da nice-a orange. Like-a da orange?"

Scornfu., the Kid pursued his quest. He entered the all-night chop-house, café, and bowling-alley of his friend and admirer, Justus O'Callahan. The O'Callahan was about in his institution, looking for leaks.

"I want it straight," said the Kid to him. "The old woman has got a hunch that she wants a peach. Now, if you've got a peach, Cal, get it out quick. I want it and others like it if you 've got 'em in plural quantities."

"The house is yours," said O'Callahan. "But there's no peach in it. It's too soon. I don't suppose you could even find 'em at one of the Broadway joints. That's too bad. When a lady fixes her mouth for a certain kind of fruit nothing else won't do. It's too late now to find any of the first-class fruiterers open. But if you think the missis would like some nice oranges, I 've just got a box of fine ones in that she might —— "

"Much obliged, Cal. It's a peach proposition right from the ring of the gong. I 'll try farther."

The time was nearly midnight as the Kid walked down the West-Side avenue. Few stores were open, and such as were practically hooted at the idea of a peach.

But in her moated flat the bride confidently awaited her Persian fruit. A champion welter-weight not find a peach ?—not stride triumphantly over the seasons and the zodiac and the almanac to fetch an Amsden's June or a Georgia cling to his owny-own ?

The Kid's eye caught sight of a window that was lighted and gorgeous with Nature's most entrancing colours. The light suddenly went out. The Kid sprinted and caught the fruiterer locking his door.

" Peaches ? " said he, with extreme deliberation.

" Well, no; sir. Not for three or four weeks yet. I haven't any idea where you might find some. There may be a few in town from under the glass, but they 'd be hard to locate. Maybe at one of the more expensive hotels— some place where there 's plenty of money to waste. I 've got some very fine oranges, though—from a shipload that came in to-day."

The Kid lingered on the corner for a moment, and then set out briskly toward a pair of green lights that flanked the steps of a building down a dark side street.

" Captain around anywhere ? " he asked of the desk sergeant of the police station.

At that moment the Captain came briskly forward from the rear. He was in plain clothes, and had a busy air.

" Hello, Kid," he said to the pugilist. " Thought you were bridal-touring ? "

"Got back yesterday. I'm a solid citizen now. Think I'll take an interest in municipal doings. How would it suit you to get into Denver Dick's place to-night, Cap?"

"Past performances," said the Captain, twisting his moustache. "Denver was closed up two months ago."

"Correct," said the Kid. "Rafferty chased him out of the Forty-third. He's running in your precinct now, and his game's bigger than ever. I'm down on this gambling business. I can put you against his game."

"In my precinct?" growled the Captain. "Are you sure, Kid? I'll take it as a favour. Have you got the entrée? How is it to be done?"

"Hammers," said the Kid. "They haven't got any steel on the doors yet. You'll need ten men. No; they won't let me in the place. Denver has been trying to do me. He thought I tipped him off for the other raid. I didn't though. You want to hurry. I've got to get back home. The house is only three blocks from here."

Before ten minutes had sped the Captain with a dozen men stole with their guide into the hallway of a dark and virtuous-looking building in which many businesses were conducted by day.

"Third floor, rear," said the Kid, softly. "I'll lead the way."

Two axemen faced the door that he pointed out to them.

" It seems all quiet," said the Captain, doubtfully. " Are you sure your tip is straight ? "

" Cut away ! " said the Kid. " It 's on me if it ain't."

The axes crashed through the as yet unprotected door. A blaze of light from within poured through the smashed panels. The door fell, and the raiders sprang into the room with their guns handy.

The big room was furnished with the gaudy magnificence dear to Denver Dick's western ideas. Various well-patronized games were in progress. About fifty men who were in the room rushed upon the police in a grand break for personal liberty. The plain-clothes men had to do a little club-swinging. More than half the patrons escaped.

Denver Dick had graced his game with his own presence that night. He led the rush that was intended to sweep away the smaller body of raiders. But when he saw the Kid his manner became personal. Being in the heavy-weight class, he cast himself joyfully upon his slighter enemy, and they rolled down a flight of stairs in each other's arms. On the landing they separated and arose, and then the Kid was able to use some of his professional tactics, which had been useless to him while in the excited clutch of a 200-pound sporting

gentleman who was about to lose $20,000 worth
of paraphernalia.

After vanquishing his adversary, the Kid
hurried upstairs and through the gambling-room
into a smaller apartment connecting by an
arched doorway.

Here was a long table set with choicest
chinaware and silver, and lavishly furnished
with food of that expensive and spectacular
sort of which the devotees of sport are supposed
to be fond. Here again was to be perceived
the liberal and florid taste of the gentleman with
the urban cognomenal prefix.

A No. 10 patent leather shoe protruded a
few of its inches outside the tablecloth along
the floor. The Kid seized this, and plucked
forth a black man in a white tie and the garb
of a servitor.

" Get up ! " commanded the Kid. " Are
you in charge of this free lunch ? "

" Yes, sah, I was. Has they done pinched
us ag'in, boss ? "

" Looks that way. Listen to me. Are
there any peaches in this layout ? If there
ain't I 'll have to throw up the sponge."

" There was three dozen, sah, when the game
opened this evinin' ; but I reckon the gentlemen
done eat 'em all up. If you 'd like to eat a
fust-rate orange, sah, I kin find you some."

" Get busy," ordered the Kid, sternly,
" and move whatever peach crop you 've got
quick, or there 'll be trouble. If anybody

oranges me again to-night, I 'll knock his face off."

The raid on Denver Dick's high-priced and prodigal luncheon revealed one lone, last peach that had escaped the epicurean jaws of the followers of chance. Into the Kid's pocket it went, and that indefatigable forager departed immediately with his prize. With scarcely a glance at the scene on the sidewalk below, where the officers were loading their prisoners into the patrol wagons, he moved homeward with long, swift strides.

His heart was light as he went. So rode the knights back to Camelot after perils and high deeds done for their ladies fair. The Kid's lady had commanded him and he had obeyed. True, it was but a peach that she had craved; but it had been no small deed to glean a peach at midnight from that wintry city where yet the February snows lay like iron. She had asked for a peach; she was his bride; in his pocket the peach was warming in his hand that held it for fear that it might fall out and be lost.

On the way the Kid turned in at an all-night drug store and said to the spectacled clerk:

"Say, sport, I wish you 'd size up this rib of mine and see if it 's broke. I was in a little scrap, and bumped down a flight or two of stairs."

The druggist made an examination.

"It isn't broken," was his diagnosis; "but

you have a bruise there that looks like you 'd
fallen off the Flatiron twice."

"That 's all right," said the Kid.   "Let 's
have your clothes-brush, please."

The bride waited in the rosy glow of the pink
lamp-shade.   The miracles were not all passed
away.   By breathing a desire for some slight
thing—a flower, a pomegranate, a—oh, yes,
a peach—she could send forth her man into
the night, into the world which could not
withstand him, and he would do her bidding.

And now he stood by her chair and laid the
peach in her hand.

"Naughty boy!" she said, fondly.   "Did
I say a peach?   I think I would much rather
have had an orange."

Blest be the bride.

THE HARBINGER

LONG before the springtide is felt in the dull bosom of the yokel does the city man know that the grass-green goddess is upon her throne. He sits at his breakfast eggs and toast, begirt by stone walls, opens his morning paper and sees journalism leave vernalism at the post.

For whereas spring's couriers were once the evidence of our finer senses, now the Associated Press does the trick.

The warble of the first robin in Hackensack, the stirring of the maple sap in Bennington, the budding of the pussy willows along Main Street in Syracuse, the first chirp of the bluebird, the swan song of the Blue Point, the annual tornado in St. Louis, the plaint of the peach pessimist from Pompton, N. J., the regular visit of the tame wild goose with a broken leg to the pond near Bilgewater Junction, the base attempt of the Drug Trust to boost the price of quinine foiled in the House by Congressman Jinks, the first tall poplar struck by lightning and the usual stunned picknickers who had taken refuge, the first crack of the ice jam in the Allegheny River, the finding of a violet in its mossy bed by the correspondent at Round Corners—these are the advance signs of the burgeoning season that are wired

into the wise city, while the farmer sees nothing
but winter upon his dreary fields.

But these be mere externals. The true
harbinger is the heart. When Strephon seeks
his Chloe and Mike his Maggie, then only is
spring arrived and the newspaper report of
the five-foot rattler killed in Squire Pettigrew's
pasture confirmed.

Ere the first violet blew, Mr. Peters, Mr.
Ragsdale and Mr. Kidd sat together on a
bench in Union Square and conspired. Mr.
Peters was the D'Artagnan of the loafers there.
He was the dingiest, the laziest, the sorriest
brown blot against the green background of
any bench in the park. But just then he was
the most important of the trio.

Mr. Peters had a wife. This had not heretofore affected his standing with Ragsy and
Kidd. But to-day it invested him with a
peculiar interest. His friends, having escaped
matrimony, had shown a disposition to deride
Mr. Peters for his venture on that troubled sea.
But at last they had been forced to acknowledge
that either he had been gifted with a large
foresight or that he was one of Fortune's
lucky sons.

For, Mrs. Peters had a dollar. A whole
dollar bill, good and receivable by the Government for customs, taxes, and all public dues.
How to get possession of that dollar was the
question up for discussion by the three musty
musketeers.

" How do you know it was a dollar ? " asked Ragsy, the immensity of the sum inclining him to scepticism.

" The coalman seen her have it," said Mr. Peters. " She went out and done some washing yesterday. And look what she give me for breakfast—the heel of a loaf and a cup of coffee, and her with a dollar ! "

" It 's fierce," said Ragsy.

" Say we go up and punch 'er and stick a towel in 'er mouth and cop the coin," suggested Kidd, viciously. " Y' ain't afraid of a woman, are you ? "

" She might holler and have us pinched," demurred Ragsy. " I don't believe in slugging no woman in a houseful of people."

" Gent'men," said Mr. Peters, severely, through his russet stubble, " remember that you are speaking of my wife. A man who would lift his hand to a lady except in the way of —— "

" Maguire," said Ragsy, pointedly, " has got his bock beer sign out. If we had a dollar we could —— "

" Hush up ! " said Mr. Peters, licking his lips. " We got to get that case note somehow, boys. Ain't what 's a man's wife's his ? Leave it to me. I 'll go over to the house and get it. Wait here for me."

" I 've seen 'em give up quick, and tell you where it 's hid if you kick 'em in the ribs," said Kidd.

" No man would kick a woman," said Peters, virtuously. " A little choking—just a touch on the windpipe—that gets away with 'em— and no marks left. Wait for me. I 'll bring back that dollar, boys."

High up in a tenement-house between Second Avenue and the river lived the Peterses in a back room so gloomy that the landlord blushed to take the rent for it. Mrs. Peters worked at sundry times, doing odd jobs of scrubbing and washing. Mr. Peters had a pure, unbroken record of five years without having earned a penny. And yet they clung together, sharing each other's hatred and misery, being creatures of habit. Of habit, the power that keeps the earth from flying to pieces ; though there is some silly theory of gravitation.

Mrs. Peters reposed her 200 pounds on the safer of the two chairs and gazed stolidly out the one window at the brick wall opposite. Her eyes were red and damp. The furniture could have been carried away on a pushcart, but no pushcart man would have removed it as a gift.

The door opened to admit Mr. Peters. His fox-terrier eyes expressed a wish. His wife's diagnosis located correctly the seat of it, but misread it hunger instead of thirst.

" You 'll get nothing more to eat till night," she said, looking out of the window again. " Take your hound-dog's face out of the room."

Mr. Peters's eye calculated the distance between them. By taking her by surprise it

might be possible to spring upon her, overthrow
her, and apply the throttling tactics of which
he had boasted to his waiting comrades. True,
it had been only a boast; never yet had he
dared to lay violent hands upon her; but
with the thoughts of the delicious, cool bock or
Culmbacher bracing his nerves, he was near to
upsetting his own theories of the treatment
due by a gentleman to a lady. But, with his
loafer's love for the more artistic and less
strenuous way, he chose diplomacy first, the
high card in the game—the assumed attitude
of success already attained.

"You have a dollar," he said, loftily, but
significantly in the tone that goes with the
lighting of a cigar—when the properties are at
hand.

"I have," said Mrs. Peters, producing the
bill from her bosom and crackling it, teasingly.

"I am offered a position in a—in a tea
store," said Mr. Peters. "I am to begin work
to-morrow. But it will be necessary for me
to buy a pair of ——"

"You are a liar," said Mrs. Peters, reinterring
the note. "No tea store, nor no A B C store,
nor no junk shop would have you. I rubbed
the skin off both me hands washin' jumpers
and overalls to make that dollar. Do you
think it come out of them suds to buy the
kind you put into you? Skiddoo! Get your
mind off of money."

Evidently the poses of Talleyrand were not

worth one hundred cents on that dollar. But diplomacy is dexterous. The artistic temperament of Mr. Peters lifted him by the straps of his congress gaiters and set him on new ground. He called up a look of desperate melancholy to his eyes.

" Clara," he said, hollowly, " to struggle further is useless. You have always misunderstood me. Heaven knows I have striven with all my might to keep my head above the waves of misfortune, but —— "

" Cut out the rainbow of hope and that stuff about walkin' one by one through the narrow isles of Spain," said Mrs. Peters, with a sigh. " I 've heard it so often. There 's an ounce bottle of carbolic on the shelf behind the empty coffee can. Drink hearty."

Mr. Peters reflected. What next ! The old expedients had failed. The two musty musketeers were awaiting him hard by the ruined château—that is to say, on a park bench with rickety cast-iron legs. His honour was at stake. He had engaged to storm the castle single-handed and bring back the treasure that was to furnish them wassail and solace. And all that stood between them and the coveted dollar was his wife, once a little girl whom he could—aha !—why not again ? Once with soft words he could, as they say, twist her around his little finger. Why not again ? Not for years had he tried it. Grim poverty and mutual hatred had killed all that. But

Ragsy and Kidd were waiting for him to bring the dollar !

Mr. Peters took a surreptitiously keen look at his wife. Her formless bulk overflowed the chair. She kept her eyes fixed out the window in a strange kind of trance. Her eyes showed that she had been recently weeping.

" I wonder," said Mr. Peters to himself, " if there 'd be anything in it."

The window was open upon its outlook of brick walls and drab, barren back yards. Except for the mildness of the air that entered, it might have been midwinter yet in the city that turns such a frowning face to besieging spring. But spring doesn't come with the thunder of cannon. She is a sapper and a miner, and you must capitulate.

" I 'll try it," said Mr. Peters to himself, making a wry face.

He went up to his wife and put his arm across her shoulders.

" Clara, darling," he said in tones that shouldn't have fooled a baby seal, " why should we have hard words ? Ain't you my own tootsum wootsums ? "

A black mark against you, Mr. Peters, in the sacred ledger of Cupid. Charges of attempted graft are filed against you, and of forgery and utterance of two of Love's holiest of appellations.

But the miracle of spring was wrought. Into the back room over the back alley between the black walls had crept the Harbinger. It was ridiculous, and yet —— Well, it is a rat-trap, and you, madam and sir and all of us, are in it.

Red and fat and crying like Niobe or Niagara, Mrs. Peters threw her arms around her lord and dissolved upon him. Mr. Peters would have striven to extricate the dollar bill from its deposit vault, but his arms were bound to his sides.

"Do you love me, James?" asked Mrs. Peters.

"Madly," said James, "but —— "

"You are ill!" exclaimed Mrs. Peters. "Why are you so pale and tired-looking?"

"I feel weak," said Mr. Peters. "I —— "

"Oh, wait; I know what it is. Wait, James. I'll be back in a minute."

With a parting hug that revived in Mr. Peters recollections of the Terrible Turk, his wife hurried out of the room and down the stairs.

Mr. Peters hitched his thumbs under his suspenders.

"All right," he confided to the ceiling. "I've got her going. I hadn't any idea the old girl was soft any more under the foolish rib. Well, sir; ain't I the Claude Melnotte of the lower East Side? What? It's a 100 to 1 shot that I get the dollar. I wonder what she went out for. I guess she's gone to tell Mrs. Muldoon on the second floor that we're reconciled. I'll remember this. Soft soap! And Ragsy was talking about slugging her!"

Mrs. Peters came back with a bottle of sarsaparilla.

"I'm glad I happened to have that dollar," she said. "You're all run down, honey."

Mr. Peters had a tablespoonful of the stuff inserted into him. Then Mrs. Peters sat on his lap and murmured:

"Call me tootsum wootsums again, James."

He sat still, held there by his materialized goddess of spring.

Spring had come.

On the bench in Union Square Mr. Ragsdale and Mr. Kidd squirmed, tongue-parched, awaiting D'Artagnan and his dollar.

"I wish I had choked her at first," said Mr. Peters to himself.

WHILE THE AUTO WAITS

PROMPTLY at the beginning of twilight came again to that quiet corner of that quiet, small park the girl in grey. She sat upon a bench and read a book, for there was yet to come a half hour in which print could be accomplished.

To repeat : Her dress was grey, and plain enough to mask its impeccancy of style and fit. A large-meshed veil imprisoned her turban hat and a face that shone through it with a calm and unconscious beauty. She had come there at the same hour on the day previous, and on the day before that ; and there was one who knew it.

The young man who knew it hovered near, relying upon burnt sacrifices to the great joss Luck. His piety was rewarded, for, in turning a page, her book slipped from her fingers and bounded from the bench a full yard away.

The young man pounced upon it with instant avidity, returning it to its owner with that air that seems to flourish in parks and public places—a compound of gallantry and hope, tempered with respect for the policeman on the beat. In a pleasant voice, he risked an inconsequent remark upon the weather—that introductory topic responsible for so much of the world's unhappiness—and stood poised for a moment, awaiting his fate.

The girl looked him over leisurely ; at his ordinary, neat dress and his features distinguished by nothing particular in the way of expression.

"You may sit down, if you like," she said, in a full, deliberate contralto. "Really, I would like to have you do so. The light is too bad for reading. I would prefer to talk."

The vassal of Luck slid upon the seat by her side with complaisance.

"Do you know," he said, speaking the formula with which park chairmen open their meetings, "that you are quite the stunningest girl I have seen in a long time ? I had my eye on you yesterday. Didn't know somebody was bowled over by those pretty lamps of yours, did you, honeysuckle ? "

"Whoever you are," said the girl, in icy tones, "you must remember that I am a lady. I will excuse the remark you have just made, because the mistake was, doubtless, not an unnatural one—in your circle. I asked you to sit down ; if the invitation must constitute me your honeysuckle, consider it withdrawn."

"I earnestly beg your pardon," pleaded the young man. His expression of satisfaction had changed to one of penitence and humility. "It was my fault, you know—I mean, there are girls, in parks, you know—that is, of course, you don't know, but —— "

"Abandon the subject, if you please. Of course I know. Now, tell me about these people passing and crowding, each way, along these paths. Where are they going ? Why do they hurry so ? Are they happy ? ''

The young man had promptly abandoned his air of coquetry. His cue was now for a waiting part ; he could not guess the rôle he would be expected to play.

" It *is* interesting to watch them," he replied, postulating her mood. " It is the wonderful drama of life. Some are going to supper and some to—er—other places. One wonders what their histories are."

" I do not," said the girl ; " I am not so inquisitive. I come here to sit because here, only, can I be near the great, common, throbbing heart of humanity. My part in life is cast where its beats are never felt. Can you surmise why I spoke to you, Mr. —— ? "

" Parkenstacker," supplied the young man. Then he looked eager and hopeful.

" No," said the girl, holding up a slender finger, and smiling slightly. " You would recognize it immediately. It is impossible to keep one's name out of print. Or even one's portrait. This veil and this hat of my maid furnish me with an *incog*. You should have seen the chauffeur stare at it when he thought I did not see. Candidly, there are five or six names that belong in the holy of holies, and mine, by the accident of birth, is one of them. I spoke to you, Mr. Stackenpot ——''

" Parkenstacker," corrected the young man, modestly.

" —Mr. Parkenstacker; because I wanted to talk, for once, with a natural man—one unspoiled by the despicable gloss of wealth and supposed social superiority. Oh! you do not know how weary I am of it—money, money, money! And of the men who surround me, dancing like little marionettes all cut by the same pattern. I am sick of pleasure, of jewels, of travel, of society, of luxuries of all kinds."

" I always had an idea," ventured the young man, hesitatingly, " that money must be a pretty good thing."

" A competence is to be desired. But when you have so many millions that —— ! " She concluded the sentence with a gesture of despair. " It is the monotony of it,". she continued, " that palls. Drives, dinners, theatres, balls, suppers, with the gilding of superfluous wealth over it all. Sometimes the very tinkle of the ice in my champagne glass nearly drives me mad."

Mr. Parkenstacker looked ingenuously interested.

" I have always liked," he said, " to read and hear about the ways of wealthy and fashionable folks. I suppose I am a bit of a snob. But I like to have my information accurate. Now, I had formed the opinion that champagne is cooled in the bottle, and not by placing ice in the glass."

The girl gave a musical laugh of genuine amusement.

"You should know," she explained, in an indulgent tone, "that we of the non-useful class depend for our amusement upon departure from precedent. Just now it is a fad to put ice in champagne. The idea was originated by a visiting Prince of Tartary while dining at the Waldorf. It will soon give way to some other whim. Just as at a dinner party this week on Madison Avenue a green kid glove was laid by the plate of each guest to be put on and used while eating olives."

"I see," admitted the young man, humbly. "These special diversions of the inner circle do not become familiar to the common public."

"Sometimes," continued the girl, acknowledging his confession of error by a slight bow, "I have thought that if I ever should love a man it would be one of lowly station. One who is a worker and not a drone. But, doubtless, the claims of caste and wealth will prove stronger than my inclination. Just now I am besieged by two. One is a Grand Duke of a German principality. I think he has, or has had, a wife, somewhere, driven mad by his intemperance and cruelty. The other is an English Marquis, so cold and mercenary that I even prefer the diabolism of the Duke. What is it that impels me to tell you these things, Mr. Packenstacker?"

" Parkenstacker," breathed the young man. " Indeed, you cannot know how much I appreciate your confidences."

The girl contemplated him with the calm, impersonal regard that befitted the difference in their stations.

" What is your line of business, Mr. Parkenstacker ? " she asked.

" A very humble one. But I hope to rise in the world. Were you really in earnest when you said that you could love a man of lowly position ? "

" Indeed I was. But I said ' might.' There is the Grand Duke and the Marquis, you know. Yes ; no calling could be too humble were the man what I would wish him to be."

" I work," declared Mr. Parkenstacker, " in a restaurant."

The girl shrank slightly.

" Not as a waiter ? " she said, a little imploringly. " Labour is noble, but—personal attendance, you know—valets and —— "

" I am not a waiter. I am cashier in "—on the street they faced that bounded the opposite side of the park was the brilliant electric sign " RESTAURANT "—" I am cashier in that restaurant you see there."

The girl consulted a tiny watch set in a bracelet of rich design upon her left wrist, and rose hurriedly. She thrust her book into a glittering reticule suspended from her waist, for which, however, the book was too large.

"Why are you not at work?" she asked.

"I am on the night turn," said the young man; "it is yet an hour before my period begins. May I not hope to see you again?"

"I do not know. Perhaps—but the whim may not seize me again. I must go quickly now. There is a dinner, and a box at the play—and, oh! the same old round. Perhaps you noticed an automobile at the upper corner of the park as you came. One with a white body."

"And red running gear?" asked the young man, knitting his brows reflectively.

"Yes. I always come in that. Pierre waits for me there. He supposes me to be shopping in the department store across the square. Conceive of the bondage of the life wherein we must deceive even our chauffeurs. Good night."

"But it is dark now," said Mr. Parkenstacker, "and the park is full of rude men. May I not walk —— ?"

"If you have the slightest regard for my wishes," said the girl, firmly, "you will remain at this bench for ten minutes after I have left. I do not mean to accuse you, but you are probably aware that autos generally bear the monogram of their owner. Again, good night."

Swift and stately she moved away through the dusk. The young man watched her graceful form as she reached the pavement at the park's edge, and turned up along it toward the corner where stood the automobile. Then he treacherously and unhesitatingly began to dodge and skim among the park trees and shrubbery in a course parallel to her route, keeping her well in sight.

When she reached the corner she turned her head to glance at the motor-car, and then passed it, continuing on across the street. Sheltered behind a convenient standing cab, the young man followed her movements closely with his eyes. Passing down the sidewalk of the street opposite the park, she entered the restaurant with the blazing sign. The place was one of those frankly glaring establishments, all white paint and glass, where one may dine cheaply and conspicuously. The girl penetrated the restaurant to some retreat at its rear, whence she quickly emerged without her hat and veil.

The cashier's desk was well to the front. A red-haired girl on the stool climbed down, glancing pointedly at the clock as she did so. The girl in grey mounted in her place.

The young man thrust his hands into his pockets and walked slowly back along the sidewalk. At the corner his foot struck a small, paper-covered volume lying there, sending it sliding to the edge of the turf. By its picturesque cover he recognized it as the book the girl had been reading. He picked it up carelessly, and saw that its title was *New*

Arabian Nights, the author being of the name
of Stevenson. He dropped it again upon the
grass, and lounged, irresolute, for a minute.
Then he stepped into the automobile, reclined
upon the cushions, and said two words to the
chauffeur :

    " Club, Henri."

A COMEDY IN RUBBER

ONE may hope, in spite of the metaphorists, to avoid the breath of the deadly upas tree; one may, by great good fortune, succeed in blacking the eye of the basilisk; one might even dodge the attentions of Cerberus and Argus; but no man, alive or dead, can escape the gaze of the Rubberer.

New York is the Caoutchouc City. There are many, of course, who go their ways, making money, without turning to the right or the left, but there is a tribe abroad wonderfully composed, like the Martians, solely of eyes and means of locomotion.

These devotees of curiosity swarm, like flies, in a moment in a struggling, breathless circle about the scene of an unusual occurrence. If a workman opens a manhole, if a street car runs over a man from North Tarrytown, if a little boy drops an egg on his way home from the grocery, if a casual house or two drops into a subway, if a lady loses a nickel through a hole in the lisle thread, if the police drag a telephone and a racing chart forth from an Ibsen Society reading-room, if Senator Depew or Mr. Chuck Connors walks out to take the air—if any of these incidents or accidents takes place, you will see the mad, irresistible rush of the " rubber " tribe to the spot.

The importance of the event does not count. They gaze with equal interest and absorption at a chorus girl or at a man painting a liver pill sign. They will form as deep a cordon around a man with a club-foot as they will around a balked automobile. They have the furor rubberendi.• They are optical gluttons, feasting and fattening on the misfortunes of their fellow-beings. They gloat and pore, and glare and squint and stare with their fishy eyes like goggle-eyed perch at the hook baited with calamity.

It would seem that Cupid would find these ocular vampires too cold game for his calorific shafts, but have we not yet to discover an immune even among the Protozoa ? Yes, beautiful Romance descended· upon two of this tribe, and love came into their hearts as they crowded about the prostrate form of a man who had been run over by a brewery wagon.

William Pry was the first on the spot. He was an expert at such gatherings. With an expression of intense happiness on his features, he stood over the victim of the accident, listening to his groans as if to the sweetest music. When the crowd of spectators had swelled to a closely-packed circle, William saw a violent commotion in the crowd opposite him. Men were hurled aside like ninepins by the impact of some moving body that clove them like the rush of a tornado. With elbows, umbrella, hat-pin, tongue, and finger-nails doing their duty, Violet Seymour forced her way through the mob of onlookers to the first row. Strong men who even had been able to secure a seat on the 5.30 Harlem express staggered back like children as she bucked centre. Two large lady spectators who had seen the Duke of Roxburgh married and had often blocked traffic on Twenty-third Street fell back into the second row with ripped shirt-waists when Violet had finished with them. William Pry loved her at first sight.

The ambulance removed the unconscious agent of Cupid. William and Violet remained after the crowd had dispersed. They were true Rubberers. People who leave the scene of an accident with the ambulance have not genuine caoutchouc in the cosmogony of their necks. The delicate, fine flavour of the affair is to be had only in the after-taste—in gloating over the spot, in gazing fixedly at the houses opposite, in hovering there in a dream more exquisite than the opium-eater's ecstasy. William Pry and Violet Seymour were connoisseurs in casualties. They knew how to extract full enjoyment from every incident.

Presently they looked at each other. Violet had a brown birthmark on her neck as large as a silver half-dollar. William fixed his eyes upon it. William Pry had inordinately bowed legs. Violet allowed her gaze to linger unswervingly

upon them. Face to face they stood thus
for moments, each staring at the other.
Etiquette would not allow them to speak ;
but in the Caoutchouc City it is permitted
to gaze without stint at the trees in the parks
and at the physical blemishes of a fellow-
creature.

At length with a sigh they parted. But
Cupid had been the driver of the brewery
wagon, and the wheel that broke a leg united
two fond hearts.

The next meeting of the hero and heroine
was in front of a board fence near Broadway.
The day had been a disappointing one.   There
had been no fights on the street, children had
kept from under the wheels of the street cars,
cripples and fat men in negligée shirts were
scarce ; nobody seemed to be inclined to slip
on banana peels or fall down with heart
disease. Even the sport from Kokomo, Ind.,
who claims to be a cousin of ex-Mayor Low
and scatters nickels from a cab window, had
not put in his appearance. There was nothing
to stare at, and William Pry had premonitions
of ennui.

But he saw a large crowd scrambling and
pushing excitedly in front of a billboard.
Sprinting for it, he knocked down an old
woman and a child carrying a bottle of milk,
and fought his way like a demon into the mass
of spectators. Already in the inner line stood
Violet Seymour with one sleeve and two

gold fillings gone, a corset steel puncture and a sprained wrist, but happy. She was looking at what there was to see. A man was painting upon the fence : " Eat Bricklets—They Fill Your Face."

Violet blushed when she saw William Pry. William jabbed a lady in a black silk raglan in the ribs, kicked a boy in the shin, hit an old gentleman on the left ear, and managed to crowd nearer to Violet. They stood for an hour looking at the man paint the letters. Then William's love could be repressed no longer. He touched her on the arm.

" Come with me," he said. " I know where there is a bootblack without an Adam's apple."

She looked up at him shyly, yet with unmistakable love transfiguring her countenance.

" And you have saved it for me ? " she asked, trembling with the first dim ecstasy of a woman beloved.

Together they hurried to the bootblack's stand. An hour they spent there gazing at the malformed youth.

A window-cleaner fell from the fifth story to the sidewalk beside them. As the ambulance came clanging up William pressed her hand joyously. " Four ribs at least and a compound fracture," he whispered, swiftly. " You are not sorry that you met me, are you, dearest ? "

" Me ? " said Violet, returning the pressure. " Sure not. I could stand all day rubbering with you."

The climax of the romance occurred a few days later. Perhaps the reader will remember the intense excitement into which the city was thrown when Eliza Jane, a coloured woman, was served with a subpœna. The Rubber Tribe encamped on the spot. With his own hands William Pry placed a board upon two beer kegs in the street opposite Eliza Jane's residence. He and Violet sat there for three days and nights. Then it occurred to a detective to open the door and serve the subpœna. He sent for a kinetoscope and did so.

Two souls with such congenial tastes could not long remain apart. As a policeman drove them away with his night stick that evening they plighted their troth. The seeds of love had been well sown, and had grown up, hardy and vigorous, into a—let us call it a rubber plant.

The wedding of William Pry and Violet Seymour was set for June 10. The Big Church in the Middle of the Block was banked high with flowers. The populous tribe of Rubberers the world over is rampant over weddings. They are the pessimists of the pews. They are the guyers of the groom and the banterers of the bride. They come to laugh at your marriage, and should you escape from Hymen's tower on the back of death's pale steed they will come to the funeral and sit in the same pew and cry over your luck. Rubber will stretch.

The church was lighted. A grosgrain carpet lay over the asphalt to the edge of the sidewalk. Bridesmaids were patting one another's sashes awry and speaking of the Bride's freckles. Coachmen tied white ribbons on their whips and bewailed the space of time between drinks. The minister was musing over his possible fee, essaying conjecture whether it would suffice to purchase a new broadcloth suit for himself and a photograph of Laura Jane Libbey for his wife. Yea, Cupid was in the air.

And outside the church, oh, my brothers, surged and heaved the rank and file of the tribe of Rubberers. In two bodies they were, with the grosgrain carpet and cops with clubs between. They crowded like cattle, they fought, they pressed and surged, and swayed and trampled one another to see a bit of a girl in a white veil acquire license to go through a man's pockets while he sleeps.

But the hour for the wedding came and went, and the bride and bridegroom came not. And impatience gave way to alarm, and alarm brought about search, and they were not found. And then two big policemen took a hand, and dragged out of the furious mob of onlookers a crushed and trampled thing, with a wedding-ring in its vest pocket, and a shredded and hysterical woman beating her way to the carpet's edge, ragged, bruised and obstreperous.

William Pry and Violet Seymour, creatures

of habit, had joined in the seething game of the spectators, unable to resist the overwhelming desire to gaze upon themselves entering, as bride and bridegroom, the rose-decked church.

Rubber will out.

ONE THOUSAND DOLLARS

" ONE thousand dollars," repeated Lawyer Tolman, solemnly and severely, " and here is the money."

Young Gillian gave a decidedly amused laugh as he fingered the thin package of new fifty-dollar notes.

" It 's such a confoundedly awkward amount," he explained, genially, to the lawyer. " If it had been ten thousand a fellow might wind up with a lot of fireworks and do himself credit. Even fifty dollars would have been less trouble."

" You heard the reading of your uncle's will," continued Lawyer Tolman, professionally dry in his tones. " I do not know if you paid much attention to its details. I must remind you of one. You are required to render to us an account of the manner of expenditure of this $1,000 as soon as you have disposed of it. The will stipulates that. I trust that you will so far comply with the late Mr. Gillian's wishes."

" You may depend upon it," said the young man, politely, " in spite of the extra expense it will entail. I may have to engage a secretary. I was never good at accounts."

Gillian went to his club. There he hunted out one whom he called Old Bryson.

Old Bryson was calm and forty and sequestered. He was in a corner reading a book, and when he saw Gillian approaching he sighed, laid down his book and took off his glasses.

"Old Bryson, wake up," said Gillian. "I've a funny story to tell you."

"I wish you would tell it to someone in the billiard-room," said Old Bryson. "You know how I hate your stories."

"This is a better one than usual," said Gillian, rolling a cigarette; "and I'm glad to tell it to you. It's too sad and funny to go with the rattling of billiard balls. I've just come from my late uncle's firm of legal corsairs. He leaves me an even thousand dollars. Now, what can a man possibly do with a thousand dollars?"

"I thought," said Old Bryson, showing as much interest as a bee shows in a vinegar cruet, "that the late Septimus Gillian was worth something like half a million."

"He was," assented Gillian, joyously, "and that's where the joke comes in. He's left his whole cargo of doubloons to a microbe. That is, part of it goes to the man who invents a new bacillus, and the rest to establish a hospital for doing away with it again. There are one or two trifling bequests on the side. The butler and the housekeeper get a seal ring and $10 each. His nephew gets $1,000."

"You've always had plenty of money to spend," observed Old Bryson.

"Tons," said Gillian. "Uncle was the fairy godmother as far as an allowance was concerned."

"Any other heirs?" asked Old Bryson.

"None." Gillian frowned at his cigarette and kicked the upholstered leather of a divan uneasily. "There is a Miss Hayden, a ward of my uncle, who lived in his house. She's a quiet thing—musical—the daughter of somebody who was unlucky enough to be his friend. I forgot to say that she was in on the seal ring and $10 joke, too. I wish I had been. Then I could have had two bottles of brut, tipped the waiter with the ring, and had the whole business off my hands. Don't be superior and insulting, Old Bryson—tell me what a fellow can do with a thousand dollars."

Old Bryson rubbed his glasses and smiled. And when Old Bryson smiled, Gillian knew that he intended to be more offensive than ever.

"A thousand dollars," he said, "means much or little. One man may buy a happy home with it and laugh at Rockefeller. Another could send his wife South with it and save her life. A thousand dollars would buy pure milk for one hundred babies during June, July, and August, and save fifty of their lives. You could count upon a half hour's diversion with it at faro in one of the fortified art galleries. It would furnish an education to an ambitious boy. I am told that a genuine Corot was secured for that amount in an auction room yesterday. You could move to a New Hampshire town and live respectably two years on it. You could rent Madison Square Garden for one evening with it, and lecture your audience, if you should have one, on the precariousness of the profession of heir presumptive."

" People might like you, Old Bryson," said Gillian, always unruffled, " if you wouldn't moralize. I asked you to tell me what I could do with a thousand dollars."

" You ? " said Bryson, with a gentle laugh. " Why, Bobby Gillian, there 's only one logical thing you could do. You can go buy Miss Lotta Lauriere a diamond pendant with the money, and then take yourself off to Idaho and inflict your presence upon a ranch. I advise a sheep ranch, as I have a particular dislike for sheep."

" Thanks," said Gillian, rising, " I thought I could depend upon you, Old Bryson. You 've hit on the very scheme. I wanted to chuck the money in a lump, for I 've got to turn in an account for it, and I hate itemizing."

Gillian phoned for a cab and said to the driver :

" The stage entrance of the Columbine Theatre."

Miss Lotta Lauriere was assisting Nature with a powder puff, almost ready for her call at a crowded matinée, when her dresser mentioned the name of Mr. Gillian.

"Let it in," said Miss Lauriere. "Now, what is it, Bobby? I'm going on in two minutes."

"Rabbit-foot your right ear a little," suggested Gillian, critically. "That's better. It won't take two minutes for me. What do you say to a little thing in the pendant line? I can stand three ciphers with a figure one in front of 'em."

"Oh, just as you say," carolled Miss Lauriere. "My right glove, Adams. Say, Bobby, did you see that necklace Della Stacey had on the other night? Twenty-two hundred dollars it cost at Tiffany's. But, of course —pull my sash a little to the left, Adams."

"Miss Lauriere for the opening chorus!" cried the call-boy without.

Gillian strolled out to where his cab was waiting.

"What would you do with a thousand dollars if you had it?" he asked the driver.

"Open a s'loon," said the cabby, promptly and huskily. "I know a place I could take money in with both hands. It's a four-story brick on a corner. I've got it figured out. Second story—Chinks and chop suey; third floor—manicures and foreign missions; fourth floor—poolroom. If you was thinking of putting up the cap——"

"Oh, no," said Gillian, "I merely asked from curiosity. I take you by the hour. Drive till I tell you to stop."

Eight blocks down Broadway Gillian poked up the trap with his cane and got out. A blind man sat upon a stool on the sidewalk selling pencils. Gillian went out and stood before him.

" Excuse me," he said, " but would you mind telling me what you would do if you had a thousand dollars ? "

" You got out of that cab that just drove up, didn't you ? " asked the blind man.

" I did," said Gillian.

" I guess you are all right," said the pencil dealer, " to ride in a cab by daylight. Take a look at that, if you like."

He drew a small book from his coat-pocket and held it out. Gillian opened it, and saw that it was a bank deposit book. It showed a balance of $1,785 to the blind man's credit.

Gillian returned the book and got into the cab.

" I forgot something," he said. " You may drive to the aw offices of Tolman & Sharp, at —— Broadway."

Lawyer Tolman looked at him hostilely and inquiringly through his gold-rimmed glasses.

" I beg your pardon," said Gillian, cheerfully, " but may I ask you a question ? It is not an impertinent one, I hope. Was Miss Hayden left anything by my uncle's will besides the ring and the $10 ? "

" Nothing," said Mr. Tolman.

" I thank you very much, sir," said Gillian,

and out he went to his cab. He gave the driver the address of his late uncle's home.

Miss Hayden was writing letters in the library. She was small and slender and clothed in black. But you would have noticed her eyes. Gillian drifted in with his air of regarding the world as inconsequent.

"I've just come from old Tolman's," he explained. "They've been going over the papers down there. They found a "—Gillian searched his memory for a legal term—"they found an amendment or a postscript or something to the will. It seemed that the old boy loosened up a little on second thoughts and willed you a thousand dollars. I was driving up this way, and Tolman asked me to bring you the money. Here it is. You'd better count it to see if it's right." Gillian laid the money beside her hand on the desk.

Miss Hayden turned white. "Oh!" she said, and again "Oh!"

Gillian half turned and looked out the window.

"I suppose, of course," he said, in a low voice, "that you know I love you."

"I am sorry," said Miss Hayden, taking up her money.

"There is no use?" asked Gillian, almost light-heartedly.

"I am sorry," she said again.

"May I write a note?" asked Gillian, with a smile. He seated himself at the big library

table. She supplied him with paper and pen
and then went back to her secretaire.

Gillian made out his account of his expenditure of the thousand dollars in these words :

" Paid by the black sheep, Robert Gillian.
$1,000 on account of the eternal happiness,
owed by Heaven to the best and dearest
woman on earth."

Gillian slipped his writing into an envelope,
bowed, and went his way.

His cab stopped again at the offices of
Tolman & Sharp.

" I have expended the thousand dollars,"
he said, cheerily, to Tolman of the gold glasses,
" and I have come to render account of it
as I agreed. There is quite a feeling of summer
in the air—do you not think so, Mr. Tolman ? "
He tossed a white envelope on the lawyer's
table. " You will find there a memorandum,
sir, of the *modus operandi* of the vanishing
of the dollars."

Without touching the envelope, Mr. Tolman
went to a door and called his partner, Sharp.
Together they explored the caverns of an
immense safe. Forth they dragged as trophy
of their search a big envelope sealed with wax.
This they forcibly invaded, and wagged their
venerable heads together over its contents.
Then Tolman became spokesman.

" Mr. Gillian," he said, formally, " there was a
codicil to your uncle's will. It was intrusted
to us privately, with instructions that it ·be

not opened until you had furnished us with a full account of your handling of the $1,000 bequest in the will. As you have fulfilled the conditions, my partner and I have read the codicil. I do not wish to encumber your understanding with its legal phraseology, but I will acquaint you with the spirit of its contents.

" In the event that your disposition of the $1,000 demonstrates that you possess any of the qualifications that deserve reward, much benefit will accrue to you. Mr. Sharp and I are named as the judges, and I assure you that we will do our duty strictly according to justice —with liberality. We are not at all unfavourably disposed toward you, Mr. Gillian. But let us return to the letter of the codicil. If your disposal of the money in question has been prudent, wise, or unselfish, it is in our power to hand you over bonds to the value of $50,000, which have been placed in our hands for that purpose. But if—as our client, the late Mr. Gillian, explicitly provides—you have used this money as you have used money in the past—I quote the late Mr. Gillian—in reprehensible dissipation among disreputable associates—the $50,000 is to be paid to Miriam Hayden, ward of the late Mr. Gillian, without delay. Now, Mr. Gillian, Mr. Sharp and I will examine your account in regard to the $1,000. You submit it in writing, I believe. I hope you will repose confidence in our decision."

Mr. Tolman reached for the envelope. Gillian

was a little the quicker in taking it up. He tore the account and its cover leisurely into strips and dropped them into his pocket.

"It's all right," he said, smilingly. "There isn't a bit of need to bother you with this. I don't suppose you'd understand these itemized bets, anyway. I lost the thousand dollars on the races. Good-day to you, gentlemen."

Tolman & Sharp shook their heads mournfully at each other when Gillian left, for they heard him whistling gaily in the hallway as he waited for the elevator.

THE DEFEAT OF THE CITY

ROBERT WALMSLEY'S descent upon the city resulted in a Kilkenny struggle. He came out of the fight victor by a fortune and a reputation. On the other hand, he was swallowed up by the city. The city gave him what he demanded, and then branded him, with its brand. It remodelled, cut, trimmed and stamped him to the pattern it approves. It opened its social gates to him, and shot him in on a close-cropped, formal lawn with the select herd of ruminants. In dress, habits, manners, provincialism, routine and narrowness he acquired that charming insolence, that irritating completeness, that sophisticated crassness, that overbalanced poise that makes the Manhattan gentleman so delightfully small in his greatness.

One of the up-state rural counties pointed with pride to the successful young metropolitan lawyer as a product of its soil. Six years earlier this county had removed the wheat straw from between its huckleberry-stained teeth, and emitted a derisive and bucolic laugh as old man Walmsley's freckle-faced " Bob " abandoned the certain three-per-dieni meals of the one-horse farm for the discontinuous quick-lunch counters of the three-ringed

metropolis. At the end of the six years no
murder trial, coaching party, automobile
accident or cotillion was complete in which
the name of Robert Walmsley did not figure.
Tailors waylaid him in the street to get a new
wrinkle from the cut of his unwrinkled trousers.
Hyphenated fellows in the clubs and members of
the oldest subpœnaed families were glad to
clap him on the back and allow him three
letters of his name.

But the Matterhorn of Robert Walmsley's
success was not scaled until he married Alicia
Van Der Pool. I cite the Matterhorn, for
just so high and cool and white and inaccessible
was this daughter of the old burghers. The
social Alps that ranged about her—over whose
bleak passes a thousand climbers struggled
—reached only to her knees. She towered in
her own atmosphere, serene, chaste, prideful,
wading in no fountains, dining no monkeys,
breeding no dogs for bench shows. She was
a Van Der Pool. Fountains were made to
play for her ; monkeys were made for other
people's ancestors ; dogs, she understood,
were created to be companions of blind persons
and objectionable characters who smoked
pipes.

This was the Matterhorn that Robert
Walmsley accomplished. If he found, with
the good poet with the game foot and artificially
curled hair, that he who ascends to mountain-
tops will find the loftiest peaks most wrapped

in clouds and snow, he concealed his chilblains beneath a brave and smiling exterior. He was a lucky man and knew it, even though he were imitating the Spartan boy with an ice-cream freezer beneath his doublet frappéeing the region of his heart.

After a brief wedding-tour abroad, the couple returned to create a decided ripple in the calm cistern (so placid and cool and sunless it is) of the best society. They entertained at their red-brick mausoleum of ancient greatness in an old square that is a cemetery of crumbled glory. And Robert Walmsley was proud of his wife ; although while one of his hands shook his guests' the other held tightly to his alpenstock and thermometer.

One day Alicia found a letter written to Robert by his mother. It was an unerudite letter, full of crops and motherly love and farm notes. It chronicled the health of the pig and the recent red calf, and asked concerning Robert's in return. It was a letter direct from the soil, straight from home, full of biographies of bees, tales of turnips, pæans of new-laid eggs, neglected parents, and the slump in dried apples.

" Why have I not been shown your mother's letters ? " asked Alicia. There was always something in her voice that made you think of lorgnettes, of accounts at Tiffany's, of sledges smoothly gliding on the trail from Dawson to Forty Mile, of the tinkling of pendant prisms on your grandmother's chandeliers, of snow lying on a convent roof ; of a police sergeant refusing bail. " Your mother," continued Alicia, " invites us to make a visit to the farm. I have never seen a farm. We will go there for a week or two, Robert."

" We will," said Robert, with the grand air of an associate Supreme Justice concurring in an opinion. " I did not lay the invitation before you because I thought you would not care to go. I am much pleased at your decision."

" I will write to her myself," answered Alicia, with a faint foreshadowing of enthusiasm. " Félice shall pack my trunks at once. Seven, I think, will be enough. I do not suppose that your mother entertains a great deal. Does she give many house parties ? "

Robert arose, and as attorney for rural places filed a demurrer against six of the seven trunks. He endeavoured to define, picture, elucidate, set forth, and describe a farm. His own words sounded strange in his ears. He had not realized how thoroughly urbsidized he had become.

A week passed, and found them landed at the little country station five hours out from the city. A grinning, stentorian, sarcastic youth driving a mule to a spring wagon hailed Robert savagely.

" Hallo, Mr. Walmsley. Found your way back at last, have you ? Sorry I couldn't bring in the automobile for you, but dad 's bull-tonguing the ten-acre clover patch with it

to-day.   Guess you 'll excuse my not wearing
a dress suit over to meet you—it ain't six
o'clock yet, you know."

" I 'm glad to see you, Tom," said Robert,
grasping his brother's hand.   " Yes, I 've found
my way at last. You 've a right to say ' at
last.' It 's been over two years since the last
time. But it will be oftener after this, my
boy."

Alicia, cool in the summer heat as an Arctic
wraith, white as a Norse snow maiden in her
flimsy muslin and fluttering lace parasol,
came round the corner of the station ; and Tom
was stripped of his assurance. He became
chiefly eyesight clothed in blue jeans, and on
the homeward drive to the mule alone did he
confide in language the inwardness of his
thoughts.

They drove homeward. The low sun dropped
a spendthrift flood of gold upon the fortunate
fields of wheat. The cities were far away.
The road lay curling around wood and dale and
hill like a ribbon lost from the robe of careless
summer. The wind followed like a whinnying
colt in the track of Phœbus's steeds.

By and by the farmhouse peeped grey out
of its faithful grove ; they saw the long lane
with its convoy of walnut trees running from
the road to the house ; they smelled the wild
rose and the breath of cool, damp willows in
the creek's bed.   And then in unison all the
voices of the soil began a chant addressed to

4

the soul of Robert Walmsley. Out of the tilted
aisles of the dim wood they came hollowly ;
they chirped and buzzed from the parched
grass ; they trilled from the ripples of the
creek ford ; they floated up in clear Pan's
pipe notes from the dimming meadows ; the
whip-poor-wills joined in as they pursued midges
in the upper air ; slow-going cow-bells struck
out a homely accompaniment—and this was
what each one said : " You 've found your
way back at last, have you ? "

The old voices of the soil spoke to him. Leaf
and bud and blossom conversed with him in
the old vocabulary of his careless youth—the
inanimate things, the familiar stones and rails,
the gates and furrows and roofs and turns of
the road had an eloquence, too, and a power in
the transformation. The country had smiled,
and he had felt the breath of it, and his heart
was drawn as if in a moment back to his old
love. The city was far away.

This rural atavism, then, seized Robert
Walmsley and possessed him. A queer thing
he noticed in connection with it was that
Alicia, sitting at his side, suddenly seemed
to him a stranger. She did not belong to this
recurrent phase. Never before had she seemed
so remote, so colourless and high—so intangible
and unreal. And yet he had never admired
her more than when she sat there by him in
the rickety spring wagon, chiming no more
with his mood and with her environment than

the Matterhorn chimes with a peasant's cabbage garden.

That night, when the greetings and the supper were over, the entire family, including Buff, the yellow dog, bestrewed itself upon the front porch. Alicia, not haughty but silent, sat in the shadow dressed in an exquisite pale-grey tea-gown. Robert's mother discoursed to her happily concerning marmalade and lumbago. Tom sat on the top step; Sisters Millie and Pam on the lowest step to catch the lightning bugs. Mother had the willow rocker. Father sat in the big arm-chair with one of its arms gone. Buff sprawled in the middle of the porch in everybody's way. The twilight pixies and pucks stole forth unseen and plunged other poignant shafts of memory into the heart of Robert. A rural madness entered his soul. The city was far away.

Father sat without his pipe, writhing in his heavy boots, a sacrifice to rigid courtesy. Robert shouted: "No, you don't!" He fetched the pipe and lit it; he seized the old gentleman's boots and tore them off. The last one slipped suddenly, and Mr. Robert Walmsley, of Washington Square, tumbled off the porch backward with Buff on top of him, howling fearfully. Tom laughed sarcastically.

Robert tore off his coat and vest and hurled them into a lilac bush.

"Come out here, you land-lubber," he cried to Tom, "and I'll put grass seed on your back.

I think you called me a ' dude ' a while ago. Come along and cut your capers."

Tom understood the invitation and accepted it with delight. Three times they wrestled on the grass, " side holds," even as the giants of the mat. And twice was Tom forced to bite grass at the hands of the distinguished lawyer. Dishevelled, panting, each still boasting of his own prowess, they stumbled back to the porch. Millie cast a pert reflection upon the qualities of a city brother. In an instant Robert had secured a horrid katydid in his fingers and bore down upon her. Screaming wildly, she fled up the lane, pursued by the avenging glass of form. A quarter of a mile and they returned, she full of apology to the victorious " dude." The rustic mania possessed him unabatedly.

" I can do up a cowpenful of you slow hayseeds," he proclaimed, vaingloriously. " Bring on your bulldogs, your hired men, and your log-rollers."

He turned hand-springs on the grass that prodded Tom to envious sarcasm. And then, with a whoop, he clattered to the rear and brought back Uncle Ike, a battered coloured retainer of the family, with his banjo, and strewed sand on the porch and danced " Chicken in the Bread Tray " and did buck-and-wing wonders for half an hour longer. Incredibly wild and boisterous things he did. He sang he told stories that set all but one shrieking he played the yokel, the humorous clodhopper; he was mad, mad with the revival of the old life in his blood.

He became so extravagant, that once his mother sought gently to reprove him. Then Alicia moved as though she were about to speak, but she did not. Through it all she sat immovable, a slim, white spirit in the dusk that no man might question or read.

By and by she asked permission to ascend to her room, saying that she was tired. On her way she passed Robert. He was standing in the door, the figure of vulgar comedy, with ruffled hair, reddened face, and unpardonable confusion of attire—no trace there of the immaculate Robert Walmsley, the courted clubman and ornament of select circles. He was doing a conjuring trick with some household utensils, and the family, now won over to him without exception, was beholding him with worshipful admiration.

As Alicia passed in Robert started suddenly. He had forgotten for the moment that she was present. Without a glance at him she went on upstairs.

After that the fun grew quiet. An hour passed in talk, and then Robert went up himself.

She was standing by the window when he entered their room. She was still clothed as when they were on the porch. Outside and crowding against the window was a giant apple tree, full blossomed.

Robert sighed and went near the window. He was ready to meet his fate. A confessed vulgarian, he foresaw the verdict of justice in the shape of that still, white-clad form. He knew the rigid lines that a Van Der Pool would draw. He was a peasant gambolling indecorously in the valley, and the pure, cold, white, unthawed summit of the Matterhorn could not but frown on him. He had been unmasked by his own actions. All the polish, the poise, the form that the city had given him had fallen from him like an ill-fitting mantle at the first breath of a country breeze. Dully he awaited the approaching condemnation.

" Robert," said the calm, cool voice of his judge, " I thought I married a gentleman."

Yes, it was coming. And yet, in the face of it, Robert Walmsley was eagerly regarding a certain branch of the apple tree upon which he used to climb out of that very window. He believed he could do it now. He wondered how many blossoms there were on the tree— ten millions ? But here was someone speaking again :

" I thought I married a gentleman," the voice went on, " but —— "

Why had she come and was standing so close by his side ?

" But I find that I have married "—was this Alicia talking ?—" something better—a man. Bob, dear, kiss me, won't you ? "

The city was far away.

THE SHOCKS OF DOOM

THERE is an aristocracy of the public parks and even of the vagabonds who use them for their private apartments. Vallance felt rather than knew this, but when he stepped down out of his world into chaos his feet brought him directly to Madison Square.

Raw and astringent as a schoolgirl—of the old order—young May breathed austerely among the budding trees. Vallance buttoned his coat, lighted his last cigarette, and took his seat upon a bench. For three minutes he mildly regretted the last hundred of his last thousand that it had cost him when the bicycle cop put an end to his last automobile ride. Then he felt in every pocket and found not a single penny. He had given up his apartment that morning. His furniture had gone toward certain debts. His clothes, save what were upon him, had descended to his man-servant for back wages. As he sat there was not in the whole city for him a bed or a broiled lobster or a street-car fare or a carnation for his buttonhole unless he should obtain them by sponging on his friends or by false pretences. Therefore he had chosen the park.

And all this was because an uncle had disinherited him, and cut down his allowance from liberality to nothing. And all that was because his nephew had disobeyed him concerning a certain girl, who comes not into this story—therefore, all readers who brush their hair toward its roots may be warned to read no further. There was another nephew, of a different branch, who had once been the prospective heir and favourite. Being without grace or hope, he had long ago disappeared in the mire. Now dragnets were out for him ; he was to be rehabilitated and restored. And so Vallance fell grandly as Lucifer to the lowest pit, joining the tattered ghosts in the little park.

Sitting there, he leaned far back on the hard bench and laughed a jet of cigarette smoke up to the lowest tree branches. The sudden severing of all his life's ties had brought him a free, thrilling, almost joyous elation. He felt precisely the sensation of the aeronaut when he cuts loose his parachute and lets his balloon drift away.

The hour was nearly ten. Not many loungers were on the benches. The park-dweller, though a stubborn fighter against autumnal coolness, is slow to attack the advance line of spring's chilly cohorts.

Then arose one from a seat near the leaping fountain, and came and sat himself at Vallance's side. He was either young or old ; cheap lodging-houses had flavoured him mustily ; razors and combs had passed him by ; in him drink had been bottled and sealed in the devil's bond. He begged a match, which is the form of introduction among park benchers, and then began to talk.

"You're not one of the regulars," he said to Vallance. "I know tailored clothes when I see 'em. You just stopped for a moment on your way through the park. Don't mind my talking to you for a while? I've got to be with somebody. I'm afraid—I'm afraid. I've told two or three of those bummers over there about it. They think I'm crazy. Say —let me tell you—all I've had to eat to-day was a couple of bretzels and an apple. To-morrow I'll stand in line to inherit three millions; and that restaurant you see over there with the autos around it will be too cheap for me to eat in. Don't believe it, do you?"

"Without the slightest trouble," said Vallance, with a laugh. "I lunched there yesterday. To-night I couldn't buy a five-cent cup of coffee."

"You don't look like one of us. Well, I guess those things happen. I used to be a high-flyer myself—some years ago. What knocked you out of the game?"

"I—oh, I lost my job," said Vallance.

"It's undiluted Hades, this city," went on the other. "One day you're eating from china, the next you are eating in China—a chop-suey joint. I've had more than my share of hard luck. For five years I've been little better than a panhandler. I was raised up to live expensively and do nothing. Say—I don't mind telling you—I 've got to talk to somebody, you see, because I 'm afraid—I 'm afraid. My name 's Ide. You wouldn't think that old Paulding, one of the millionaïres on Riverside Drive, was my uncle, would you ? Well, he is. I lived in his house once, and had all the money I wanted. Say, haven't you got the price of a couple of drinks about you—er—what 's your name ——''

"Dawson," said Vallance. "No ; I 'm sorry to say that I 'm all in, financially."

"I 've been living for a week in a coal cellar on Division Street," went on Ide, "with a crook they called ' Blinky ' Morris. I didn't have anywhere else to go. While I was out to-day a chap with some papers in his pocket was there, asking for me. I didn't know but what he was a fly cop, so I didn't go around again till after dark. There was a letter there he had left for me. Say— Dawson, it was from a big down-town lawyer, Mead. I 've seen his sign on Ann Street. Paulding wants me to play the prodigal nephew —wants me to come back and be his heir again and blow in his money. I 'm to call at the lawyer's office at ten to-morrow and step into my old shoes again—heir to three million, Dawson, and $10,000 a year pocket money. And—I 'm afraid—I 'm afraid."

The vagrant leaped to his feet and raised

both trembling arms above his head. He caught his breath and moaned hysterically.

Vallance seized his arm and forced him back to the bench.

" Be quiet ! " he commanded, with something like disgust in his tones. " One would think you had lost a fortune, instead of being about to acquire one. Of what are you afraid ? "

Ide cowered and shivered on the bench. He clung to Vallance's sleeve, and even in the dim glow of the Broadway lights the latest disinherited one could see drops on the other's brow wrung out by some strange terror.

" Why, I 'm afraid something will happen to me before morning. I don't know what— something to keep me from coming into that money. I 'm afraid a tree will fall on me— I 'm afraid a cab will run over me, or a stone drop on me from a housetop, or something. I never was afraid before. I 've sat in this park a hundred nights as calm as a graven image without knowing where my breakfast was to come from. But now it 's different. I love money, Dawson—I 'm happy as a god when it 's trickling through my fingers, and people are bowing to me, with the music and the flowers and fine clothes all around. As long as I knew I was out of the game I didn't mind. I was even happy sitting here ragged and hungry, listening to the fountain jump and watching the carriages go up the avenue. But it 's in reach of my hand again now—

almost—and I can't stand it to wait twelve hours, Dawson—I can't stand it. There are fifty things that could happen to me—I could go blind—I might be attacked with heart disease—the world might come to an end before I could —— "

Ide sprang to his feet again, with a shriek. People stirred on the benches and began to look. Vallance took his arm.

"Come and walk," he said, soothingly. "And try to calm yourself. There is no need to become excited or alarmed. Nothing is going to happen to you. One night is like another."

"That's right," said Ide. "Stay with me, Dawson—that's a good fellow. Walk around with me awhile. I never went to pieces like this before, and I've had a good many hard knocks. Do you think you could hustle something in the way of a little lunch, old man? I'm afraid my nerve's too far gone to try any panhandling."

Vallance led his companion up almost deserted Fifth Avenue, and then westward along the Thirties toward Broadway. "Wait here a few minutes," he said, leaving Ide in a quiet and shadowed spot. He entered a familiar hotel, and strolled toward the bar quite in his old assured way.

"There's a poor devil outside, Jimmy," he said to the bar-tender, "who says he's hungry, and looks it. You know what they do when you give them money. Fix up a sandwich or two for him ; and I 'll see that he doesn't throw it away."

"Certainly, Mr. Vallance," said the bar-tender. "They ain't all fakes. Don't like to see anybody go hungry."

He folded a liberal supply of the free lunch into a napkin. Vallance went with it and joined his companion. Ide pounced upon the food ravenously. "I haven't had any free lunch as good as this in a year," he said. "Aren't you going to eat any, Dawson ? "

"I 'm not hungry—thanks," said Vallance.

"We 'll go back to the Square," said Ide. "The cops won't bother us there. I 'll roll up the rest of this ham and stuff for our breakfast. I won't eat any more. I 'm afraid I 'll get sick. Suppose I 'd die of cramps or something to-night, and never get to touch that money again ! It 's eleven hours yet till time to see that lawyer. You won't leave me, will you, Dawson ? I 'm afraid something might happen. You haven't any place to go, have you ? "

"No," said Vallance, "nowhere to-night. I 'll have a bench with you."

"You take it cool," said Ide, "if you 've told it to me straight. I should think a man put on the bum from a good job just in one day would be tearing his hair."

"I believe I 've already remarked," said Vallance, laughing, "that I would have thought that a man who was expecting to come into a fortune on the next day would be feeling pretty easy and quiet."

" It 's funny business," philosophized Ide, " about the way people take things, anyhow. Here 's your bench, Dawson, right next to mine. The light don't shine in your eyes here. Say, Dawson, I 'll get the old man to give you a letter to somebody about a job when I get back home. You 've helped me a lot to-night. I don't believe I could have gone through the night if I hadn't struck you."

" Thank you," said Vallance. " Do you lie down or sit up on these when you sleep ? "

For hours Vallance gazed almost without winking at the stars through the branches of the trees, and listened to the sharp slapping of horses' hoofs on the sea of asphalt to the south. His mind was active, but his feelings were dormant. Every emotion seemed to have been eradicated. He felt no regrets, no fears, no pain or discomfort. Even when he thought of the girl, it was as of an inhabitant of one of those remote stars at which he gazed. He remembered the absurd antics of his companion and laughed softly, yet without a feeling of mirth. Soon the daily army of milk wagons made of the city a roaring drum to which they marched. Vallance fell asleep on his comfortless bench.

At ten o'clock the next day the two stood at the door of Lawyer Mead's office in Ann Street.

Ide's nerves fluttered worse than ever when

the hour approached ; and Vallance could not
decide to leave him a possible prey to the
dangers he dreaded.

When they entered the office, Lawyer Mead
looked at them wonderingly. He and Vallance
were old friends. After his greeting, he turned
to Ide, who stood with white face and trembling
limbs before the expected crisis.

" I sent a second letter to your address last
night, Mr. Ide," he said. " I learned this
morning that you were not there to receive it.
It will inform you that Mr. Paulding has
reconsidered his offer to take you back into
favour. He has decided not to do so, and
desires you to understand that no change will
be made in the relations existing between you
and him."

Ide's trembling suddenly ceased. The colour
came back to his face, and he straightened his
back. His jaw went forward half an inch, and
a gleam came into his eye. He pushed back
his battered hat with one hand, and extended
the other, with levelled fingers, toward the
lawyer. He took a long breath and then
laughed sardonically.

" Tell old Paulding he may go to the devil,"
he said, loudly and clearly, and turned and
walked out of the office with a firm and lively
step.

Lawyer Mead turned on his heel to Vallance
and smiled.

" I am glad you came in," he said, genially.

" Your uncle wants you to return home at once. He is reconciled to the situation that led to his hasty action, and desires to say that all will be as —— "

" Hey, Adams ! " cried Lawyer Mead, breaking his sentence, and calling to his clerk. " Bring a glass of water—Mr. Vallance has fainted."

THE PLUTONIAN FIRE

THERE are a few editor men with whom I am
privileged to come in contact. It has not been
long since it was their habit to come in contact
with me. There is a difference.

They tell me that with a large number of
the manuscripts that are submitted to them
come advices (in the way of a boost) from the
author asseverating that the incidents in the
story are true. The destination of such
contributions depends wholly upon the question
of the enclosure of stamps. Some are returned,
the rest are thrown on the floor in a corner on
top of a pair of gum shoes, an over-turned
statuette of the Winged Victory, and a pile of
old magazines containing a picture of the
editor in the act of reading the latest copy of
Le Petit Journal, right side up—you can tell
by the illustrations. It is only a legend that
there are waste baskets in editors' offices.

Thus is truth held in disrepute. But in
time truth and science and nature will adapt
themselves to art. Things will happen logically,
and the villain be discomfited instead of being
elected to the board of directors. But in the
meantime fiction must not only be divorced
from fact, but must pay alimony and be
awarded custody of the press dispatches.

This preamble is to warn you off the grade crossing of a true story. Being that, it shall be told simply, with conjunctions substituted for adjectives wherever possible, and whatever evidences of style may appear in it shall be due to the linotype man. It is a story of the literary life in a great city, and it should be of interest to every author within a 20-mile radius of Gosport, Ind., whose desk holds a MS. story beginning thus : " While the cheers following his nomination were still ringing through the old court-house, Harwood broke away from the congratulating handclasps of his henchmen, and hurried to Judge Creswell's house to find Ida."

Pettit came up out of Alabama to write fiction. The Southern papers had printed eight of his stories under an editorial caption identifying the author as the son of " the gallant Major Pettingill Pettit, our former County Attorney, and hero of the Battle of Look-out Mountain."

Pettit was a rugged fellow, with a kind of shamefaced culture, and my good friend. His father kept a general store in a little town called Hosea. Pettit had been raised in the pine-woods and broom-sedge fields adjacent thereto. He had in his gripsack two manuscript novels of the adventures in Picardy of one Gaston Laboulaye, Vicompte de Montrepos, in the year 1329. That's nothing. We all do that. And some day, when we make a hit with the

little sketch about a newsy and his lame dog,
the editor prints the other one for us—or
" on us," as the saying is—and then—and then
we have to get a big valise and peddle those
patent air-draft gas-burners. At $1.25
everybody should have 'em.

I took Pettit to the red-brick house which
was to appear in an article entitled " Literary
Landmarks of Old New York," some day when
we got through with it. He engaged a room
there, drawing on the general store for his
expenses. I showed New York to him, and he
did not mention how much narrower Broadway
is than Lee Avenue in Hosea. This seemed
a good sign, so I put the final test.

" Suppose you try your hand at a descriptive
article," I suggested, " giving your impressions
of New York as seen from the Brooklyn Bridge.
The fresh point of view, the —— "

" Don't be a fool," said Pettit. " Let 's
go have some beer. On the whole, I rather
like the city."

We discovered and enjoyed the only true
Bohemia. Every day and night we repaired
to one of those palaces of marble and glass and
tilework, where goes on a tremendous and
sounding epic of life. Valhalla itself could not
be more glorious and sonorous. The classic
marble on which we ate, the great, light-flooded
vitreous front, adorned with snow-white scrolls ;
the grand Wagnerian din of clanking cups
and bowls, the flashing staccato of brandishing

cutlery, the piercing recitative of the white-aproned grub-maidens at the morgue-like banquet tables; the recurrent lied-motif of the cash-register—it was a gigantic, triumphant welding of art and sound, a deafening, soul-uplifting pageant of heroic and emblematic life. And the beans were only ten cents. We wondered why our fellow-artists cared to dine at sad little tables in their so-called Bohemian restaurants; and we shuddered lest they should seek out our resorts and make them conspicuous with their presence.

Pettit wrote many stories, which the editors returned to him. He wrote love stories, a thing I have always kept free from, holding the belief that the well-known and popular sentiment is not properly a matter for publication, but something to be privately handled by the alienists and florists. But the editors had told him that they wanted love stories, because they said the women read them.

Now, the editors are wrong about that, of course. Women do not read the love stories in the magazines. They read the poker-game stories and the recipes for cucumber lotion. The love stories are read by fat cigar drummers and little ten-year-old girls. I am not criticising the judgment of editors. They are mostly very fine men, but a man can be but one man, with individual opinions and tastes. I knew two associate editors of a magazine who were wonderfully alike in almost everything.

And yet one of them was very fond of Flaubert, while the other preferred gin.

Pettit brought me his returned manuscripts, and we looked them over together to find out why they were not accepted. They seemed to me pretty fair stories, written in a good style, and ended, as they should, at the bottom of the last page.

They were well constructed, and the events were marshalled in orderly and logical sequence. But I thought I detected a lack of living substance—it was much as if I gazed at a symmetrical array of presentable clamshells from which the succulent and vital inhabitants had been removed. I intimated that the author might do well to get better acquainted with his theme.

" You sold a story last week," said Pettit, " about a gun fight in an Arizona mining town in which the hero drew his Colt's .45 and shot seven bandits as fast as they came in the door. Now, if a six-shooter could —— "

" Oh, well," said I, " that 's different. Arizona is a long way from New York. I could have a man stabbed with a lariat or chased by a pair of chaparreras if I wanted to, and it wouldn't be noticed until the usual error-sharp from around McAdams Junction isolates the erratum and writes in to the papers about it. But you are up against another proposition. This thing they call love is as common around New York as it is in Sheboygan during the young onion season. It may be mixed here with a little commercialism—they read Byron, but they look up Bradstreet's, too, while they 're among the B's, and Brigham also if they have time—but it 's pretty much the same old internal disturbance everywhere. You can fool an editor with a fake picture of a cowboy mounting a pony with his left hand on the saddle-horn, but you can't put him up a tree with a love story. So you 've got to fall in love and then write the real thing."

Pettit did. I never knew whether he was taking my advice or whether he fell an accidental victim.

There was a girl he had met at one of these studio contrivances—a glorious, impudent, lucid, open-minded girl with hair the colour of Culmbacher, and a good-natured way of despising you. She was a New York girl.

Well (as the narrative style permits us to say infrequently), Pettit went to pieces. All those pains, those lover's doubts, those heart-burnings and tremors of which he had written so unconvincingly were his. Talk about Shylock's pound of flesh ! Twenty-five pounds Cupid got from Pettit. Which is the usurer ?

One night Pettit came to my room exalted. Pale and haggard, but exalted. She had given him a jonquil.

" Old Hoss," said he, with a new smile flickering around his mouth, " I believe I could write that story to-night—the one, you know, that is to win out. I can feel it. I don't know whether it will come out or not, but I can feel it."

I pushed him out of my door. " Go to your room and write it," I ordered. " Else I can see your finish. I told you this must come first. Write it to-night, and put it under my door when it is done. Put it under my door to-night when it is finished—don't keep it until to-morrow."

I was reading my bully old pal Montaigne at two o'clock, when I heard the sheets rustle under my door. I gathered them up and read the story.

The hissing of geese, the languishing cooing of doves, the braying of donkeys, the chatter of irresponsible sparrows—these were in my mind's ear as I read. " Suffering Sappho ! " I exclaimed to myself. " Is this the divine fire that is supposed to ignite genius, and make it practicable and wage-earning ? "

The story was sentimental drivel, full of whimpering soft-heartedness and gushing egoism. All the art that Pettit had acquired was gone. A perusal of its buttery phrases would have made a cynic of a sighing chamber-maid.

In the morning Pettit came to my room. I read him his doom mercilessly. He laughed idiotically.

" All right, Old Hoss," he said, cheerily, " make cigar-lighters of it. What 's the

difference ?   I 'm going to take her to lunch
at Claremont to-day."

There was about a month of it. And then
Pettit came to me bearing an invisible mitten,
with the fortitude of a dish-rag. He talked
of the grave and South America and prussic
acid ; and I lost an afternoon getting him
straight. I took him out, and saw that large
and curative doses of whisky were administered
to him. I warned you this was a true story—
'ware your white ribbons if you follow this
tale. For two weeks I fed him whisky and
Omar, and read to him regularly every evening
the column in the evening paper that reveals
the secrets of female beauty. I recommend
the treatment.

After Pettit was cured he wrote more stories.
He recovered his old-time facility, and did
work just short of good enough. Then the
curtain rose on the third act.

A little, dark-eyed, silent girl from New
Hampshire, who was studying applied design,
fell deeply in love with him. She was the
intense sort, but externally *glacé*, such as New
England sometimes fools us with. Pettit
liked her mildly, and took her about a good
deal. She worshipped him, and now and then
bored him.

There came a climax when she tried to jump
out of a window, and he had to save her by
some perfunctory, unmeant wooing. Even I
was shaken by the depths of the absorbing

affection she showed. Home, friends, traditions, creeds went up like thistle-down in the scale against her love. It was really discomposing.

One night again Pettit sauntered in, yawning. As he had told me before, he said he felt that he could do a great story, and as before I hunted him to his room and saw him open his inkstand. At one o'clock the sheets of paper slid under my door.

I read that story, and I jumped up, late as it was, with a whoop of joy. Old Pettit had done it. Just as though it lay there, red and bleeding, a woman's heart was written into the lines. You couldn't see the joining, but art, exquisite art, and pulsing nature had been combined into a love story that took you by the throat like the quinsy. I broke into Pettit's room and beat him on the back and called him names —names high up in the galaxy of the immortals that we admired. And Pettit yawned and begged to be allowed to sleep.

On the morrow I dragged him to an editor. The great man read, and, rising, gave Pettit his hand. That was a decoration, a wreath of bay, and a guarantee of rent.

And then old Pettit smiled slowly. I call him Gentleman Pettit now to myself. It's a miserable name to give a man, but it sounds better than it looks in print.

" I see," said old Pettit, as he took up his story and began tearing it into small strips,

" I see the game now. You can't write with ink, and you can't write with your own heart's blood, but you can write with the heart's blood of someone else.   You have to be a cad before you can be an artist. Well, I am for old Alabam and the Major's store.   Have you got a light, Old Hoss ? "

I went with Pettit to the depôt and died hard.

" Shakespeare's sonnets ? " I blurted, making a last stand.   " How about him ? "

" A cad," said Pettit.   " They give it to you, and you sell it—love, you know. I 'd rather sell ploughs for father."

" But," I protested, " you are reversing the decision of the world's greatest —— "

" Good-bye, Old Hoss," said Pettit.

" Critics," I continued.   " But—say--if the Major can use a fairly good salesman and book-keeper down there in the store, let me know, will you ? "

NEMESIS AND THE CANDY MAN

"WE sail at eight in the morning on the *Celtic*," said Honoria, plucking a loose thread from her lace sleeve.

"I heard so," said young Ives, dropping his hat, and muffing it as he tried to catch it, "and I came around to wish you a pleasant voyage."

"Of course you heard it," said Honoria, coldly sweet, "since we have had no opportunity of informing you ourselves."

Ives looked at her pleadingly, but with little hope.

Outside in the street a high-pitched voice chanted, not unmusically, a commercial gamut of "Cand-ee-ee-ee-s! Nice, fresh cand-ee-ee-ee-ees!"

"It's our old candy man," said Honoria, leaning out the window and beckoning. "I want some of his motto kisses. There's nothing in the Broadway shops half so good."

The candy man stopped his pushcart in front of the old Madison Avenue home. He had a holiday and festival air unusual to street peddlers. His tie was new and bright red, and a horseshoe pin, almost life-size, glittered speciously from its folds. His brown, thin face was crinkled into a semi-foolish smile.

Striped cuffs with dog-head buttons covered the tan on his wrists.

" I do believe he 's going to get married," said Honoria, pityingly. " I never saw him taken that way before. And to-day is the first time in months that he has cried his wares, I am sure."

Ives threw a coin to the sidewalk. The candy man knows his customers. He filled a paper bag, climbed the old-fashioned stoop, and handed it in.

" I remember —— " said Ives.

" Wait," said Honoria.

She took a small portfolio from the drawer of a writing-desk, and from the portfolio a slip of flimsy paper one-quarter of an inch by two inches in size.

" This," said Honoria, inflexibly, " was wrapped about the first one we opened."

" It was a year ago," apologized Ives, as he held out his hand for it—

> " As long as skies above are blue
> To you, my love, I will be true."

This he read from the slip of flimsy paper.

" We were to have sailed a fortnight ago," said Honoria, gossipingly. " It has been such a warm summer. The town is quite deserted. There is nowhere to go. Yet I am told that one or two of the roof gardens are amusing. The singing—and the dancing—on one or two seem to have met with approval."

Ives did not wince. When you are in the ring you are not surprised when your adversary taps you on the ribs.

" I followed the candy man that time," said Ives, irrelevantly, " and gave him five dollars at the corner of Broadway."

He reached for the paper bag in Honoria's lap, took out one of the square, wrapped confections, and slowly unrolled it.

" Sara Chillingworth's father," said Honoria, " has given her an automobile."

" Read that," said Ives, handing over the slip that had been wrapped around the square of candy.

> " Life teaches us—how to live,
>   Love teaches us—to forgive."

Honoria's cheeks turned pink.

" Honoria ! " cried Ives, starting up from his chair.

" Miss Clinton," corrected Honoria, rising like Venus from the bead on the surf. " I warned you not to speak that name again."

" Honoria," repeated Ives, " you must hear me. I know I do not deserve your forgiveness, but I must have it. There is a madness that possesses one sometimes for which his better nature is not responsible. I throw everything else but you to the winds. I strike off the chains that have bound me. I renounce the siren that lured me from you. Let the bought verse of that street peddler plead for me. It

is you only whom I can love. Let your love
forgive, and I swear to you that mine will be
true ' as long as skies above are blue.' ''

*   *   *   *

On the west side, between Sixth and Seventh
Avenues, an alley cuts the block in the middle.
It perishes in a little court in the centre of
the block. The district is theatrical ; the
inhabitants the bubbling froth of half a dozen
nations. The atmosphere is Bohemian, the
language polyglot, the locality precarious.

In the court at the rear of the alley lived the
candy man. At seven o'clock he pushed his
cart into the narrow entrance, rested it upon
the irregular stone slats, and sat upon one of
the handles to cool himself. There was a great
draught of cool wind through the alley.

There was a window above the spot where
he always stopped his pushcart. In the cool
of the afternoon Mlle. Adèle, drawing card
of the Aerial Roof Garden, sat at the window
and took the air. Generally her ponderous
mass of dark auburn hair was down, that the
breeze might have the felicity of aiding Sidonie,
the maid, in drying and airing it. About her
shoulders—the point of her that the photo-
graphers always made the most of—was loosely
draped a heliotrope scarf. Her arms to the
elbow were bare—there were no sculptors there
to rave over them—but even the stolid bricks
in the walls of the alley should not have been
so insensate as to disapprove. While she sat

thus Félice, another maid, anointed and bathed the small feet that twinkled and so charmed the nightly Aerial audiences.

Gradually Mademoiselle began to notice the candy man stopping to mop his brow and cool himself beneath her window. In the hands of her maids she was deprived for the time of her vocation—the charming and binding to her chariot of man. To lose time was displeasing to Mademoiselle. Here was the candy man—no fit game for her darts, truly—but of the sex upon which she had been born to make war.

After casting upon him looks of unseeing coldness for a dozen times, one afternoon she suddenly thawed, and poured down upon him a smile that put to shame the sweets upon his cart.

"Candy man," she said, cooingly, while Sidonie followed her impulsive dive, brushing the heavy auburn hair, "don't you think I am beautiful ? "

The candy man laughed harshly, and looked up, with his thin jaw set, while he wiped his forehead with a red-and-blue handkerchief.

"Yer 'd make a dandy magazine cover," he said, grudgingly. "Beautiful or not is for them that cares. It 's not my line. If yer lookin' for bouquets apply elsewhere between nine and twelve. I think we 'll have rain."

Truly, fascinating a candy man is like killing rabbits in a deep snow ; but the hunter's

blood is widely diffused.   Mademoiselle tugged
a great coil of hair from Sidonie's hands and
let it fall out the window.

"Candy man, have you a sweetheart anywhere with hair as long and soft as that?
And with an arm so round?"   She flexed
an arm like Galatea's after the miracle across
the window-sill.

The candy man cackled shrilly as he arranged
a stock of butter-scotch that had tumbled
down.

"Smoke up!" said he, vulgarly.   "Nothin'
doin' in the complimentary line.   I'm too
wise to be bamboozled by a switch of hair and
a newly-massaged arm.   Oh, I guess you'll
make good in the calcium, all right, with plenty
of powder and paint on and the orchestra
playing ' Under the Old Apple Tree.'   But don't
put on your hat and chase downstairs to fly
to the Little Church Around the Corner with
me.   I've been up against peroxide and make-
up boxes before.   Say, all joking aside—don't
you think we'll have rain? "

"Candy man," said Mademoiselle, softly,
with her lips curving and her chin dimpling,
"don't you think I'm pretty? "

The candy man grinned.

"Savin' money, ain't yer? " said he, " by
bein' yer own press agent.   I smoke, but I
haven't seen yer mug on any of the five-cent
cigar boxes.   It 'd take a new brand of woman
to get me goin', anyway.   I know 'em from

side-combs to shoe-laces. Gimme a good day's
sales and steak-and-onions at seven, and a pipe
and an evenin' paper back there in the court,
and I 'll not trouble Lillian Russell herself to
wink at me, if you please."

Mademoiselle pouted.

" Candy man," she said, softly and deeply,
" yet you shall say that I am beautiful. All
men say so, and so shall you."

The candy man laughed and pulled out his
pipe.

" Well," said he, " I must be goin' in.
There is a story in the evenin' paper that I am
readin'. Men are divin' in the seas for a
treasure, and pirates are watchin' them from
behind a reef. And there ain't a woman on
land or water or in the air. Good evenin'."
And he trundled his pushcart down the
alley and back to the musty court where he
lived.

Incredibly to him who has not learned
woman, Mademoiselle sat at the window each
day and spread her nets for the ignominious
game. Once she kept a grand cavalier waiting
in her reception chamber for half an hour while
she battered in vain the candy man's tough
philosophy. His rough laugh chafed her vanity
to its core. Daily he sat on his cart in the
breeze of the alley while her hair was being
ministered to, and daily the shafts of her beauty
rebounded from his dull bosom pointless and
ineffectual. Unworthy pique brightened her

eyes. Pride-hurt, she glowed upon him in a
way that would have sent her higher adorers
into an egoistic paradise. The candy man's
hard eyes looked upon her with a half-concealed
derision that urged her to the use of the sharpest
arrow in her beauty's quiver.

One afternoon she leaned far over the sill,
and she did not challenge and torment him as
usual.

" Candy man," said she, " stand up and look
into my eyes."

He stood up and looked into her eyes, with
his harsh laugh like the sawing of wood. He
took out his pipe, fumbled with it, and put it
back into his pocket with a trembling hand.

" That will do," said Mademoiselle, with a
slow smile. " I must go now to my *masseuse*.
Good evening."

The next evening at seven the candy man
came and rested his cart under the window.
But was it the candy man ? His clothes were
a bright new check. His necktie was a flaming
red, adorned by a glittering horseshoe pin,
almost life-size. His shoes were polished ;
the tan of his cheeks had paled—his hands
had been washed. The window was empty
and he waited under it with his nose upward
like a hound hoping for a bone.

Mademoiselle came, with Sidonie carrying
her load of hair. She looked at the candy
man and smiled, a slow smile that faded away
into ennui. Instantly she knew that the game

was bagged ; and so quickly she wearied of the chase. She began to talk to Sidonie.

"Been a fine day," said the candy man, hollowly. "First time in a month I've felt first-class. Hit it up down old Madison, hollering out like I useter. Think it 'll rain to-morrow ? "

Mademoiselle laid two round arms on the cushion on the window-sill, and a dimpled chin upon them.

"Candy man," said she, softly, "do you not love me ? "

The candy man stood up and leaned against the brick wall.

"Lady," said he, chokingly, "I've got $800 saved up. Did I say you wasn't beautiful ? Take it every bit of it, and buy a collar for your dog with it."

A sound as of a hundred silvery bells tinkled in the room of Mademoiselle. The laughter filled the alley and trickled back into the court, as strange a thing to enter there as sunlight itself. Mademoiselle was amused. Sidonie, a wise echo, added a sepulchral but faithful contralto. The laughter of the two seemed at last to penetrate the candy man. He fumbled with his horseshoe pin. At length Mademoiselle, exhausted, turned her flushed, beautiful face to the window.

"Candy man," said she, "go away. When I laugh Sidonie pulls my hair. I can but laugh while you remain there."

"Here is a note for Mademoiselle," said Félice, coming to the window in the room.

"There is no justice," said the candy man, lifting the handle of his cart and moving away.

Three yards he moved, and stopped. Loud shriek after shriek came from the window of Mademoiselle. Quickly he ran back. He heard a body thumping upon the floor and a sound as though heels beat alternately upon it.

"What is it?" he called.

Sidonie's severe head came into the window.

"Mademoiselle is overcome by bad news," she said. "One whom she loved with all her soul has gone—you may have heard of him —he is Monsieur Ives. He sails across the ocean to-morrow. Oh, you men!"

SQUARING THE CIRCLE

AT the hazard of wearying you this tale of vehement emotions must be prefaced by a discourse on geometry.

Nature moves in circles; Art in straight lines. The natural is rounded; the artificial is made up of angles. A man lost in the snow wanders, in spite of himself, in perfect circles; the city man's feet, denaturalized by rectangular streets and floors, carry him ever away from himself.

The round eyes of childhood typify innocence; the narrowed line of the flirt's optic proves the invasion of art. The horizontal mouth is the mark of determined cunning; who has not read Nature's most spontaneous lyric in lips rounded for the candid kiss?

Beauty is Nature in perfection; circularity is its chief attribute. Behold the full moon, the enchanting golf ball, the domes of splendid temples, the huckleberry pie, the wedding ring, the circus ring, the ring for the waiter, and the " round " of drinks.

On the other hand, straight lines show that Nature has been deflected. Imagine Venus's girdle transformed into a " straight front " !

When we begin to move in straight lines and turn sharp corners our natures begin to change. The consequence is that Nature, being more adaptive than Art, tries to conform to its sterner regulations. The result is often a rather curious product—for instance : A prize chrysanthemum, wood alcohol whisky, a Republican Missouri, cauliflower *au gratin*, and a New Yorker.

Nature is lost quickest in a big city. The cause is geometrical, not moral. The straight lines of its streets and architecture, the rectangularity of its laws and social customs, the undeviating pavements, the hard, severe, depressing, uncompromising rules of all its ways—even of its recreation and sports—coldly exhibit a sneering defiance of the curved line of Nature.

Wherefore, it may be said that the big city has demonstrated the problem of squaring the circle. And it may be added that this mathematical introduction precedes an account of the fate of a Kentucky feud that was imported to the city, that has a habit of making its importations conform to its angles.

The feud began in the Cumberland Mountains between the Folwell and the Harkness families. The first victim of the homespun vendetta was a 'possum dog belonging to Bill Harkness. The Harkness family evened up this dire loss by laying out the chief of the Folwell clan. The Folwells were prompt at repartee. They oiled up their squirrel rifles and made it feasible for Bill Harkness to follow his dog to a land

where the 'possums come down when treed
without the stroke of an axe.

The feud flourished for forty years.
Harknesses were shot at the plough, through
their lamp-lit cabin windows, coming from
camp-meeting, asleep, in duello, sober and
otherwise, singly and in family groups, prepared
and unprepared. Folwells had the branches
of their family tree lopped off in similar ways,
as the traditions of their country prescribed
and authorized.

By and by the pruning left but a single
member of each family. And then Cal
Harkness, probably reasoning that further
pursuance of the controversy would give a
too decided personal flavour to the feud,
suddenly disappeared from the relieved
Cumberlands, baulking the avenging hand of
Sam, the ultimate opposing Folwell.

A year afterward Sam Folwell learned that
his hereditary, unsuppressed enemy was living
in New York City. Sam turned over the big
iron wash-pot in the yard, scraped off some of
the soot, which he mixed with lard and shined
his boots with the compound. He put on his
store clothes of butternut dyed black, a white
shirt and collar, and packed a carpet-sack
with Spartan *lingerie*. He took his squirrel
rifle from its hooks, but put it back again
with a sigh. However ethical and plausible
the habit might be in the Cumberlands, perhaps
New York would not swallow his pose of hunting

squirrels among the sky-scrapers along Broadway. An ancient but reliable Colt's revolver that he resurrected from a bureau drawer seemed to proclaim itself the pink of weapons for metropolitan adventure and vengeance. This and a hunting-knife in a leather sheath Sam packed in the carpet-sack. As he started, muleback, for the lowland railroad station the last Folwell turned in his saddle and looked grimly at the little cluster of white-pine slabs in the clump of cedars that marked the Folwell burying-ground.

Sam Folwell arrived in New York in the night. Still moving and living in the free circles of Nature, he did not perceive the formidable, pitiless, restless, fierce angles of the great city waiting in the dark to close about the rotundity of his heart and brain and mould him to the form of its millions of re-shaped victims. A cabby picked him out of the whirl, as Sam himself had often picked a nut from a bed of wind-tossed autumn leaves, and whisked him away to a hotel commensurate to his boots and carpet-sack.

On the next morning the last of the Folwells made his sortie into the city that sheltered the last Harkness. The Colt was thrust beneath his coat and secured by a narrow leather belt; the hunting-knife hung between his shoulder-blades, with the haft an inch below his coat collar. He knew this much—that Cal Harkness drove an express wagon somewhere in that town, and that he, Sam Folwell, had come to kill him.   And as he stepped upon the sidewalk the red came into his eye and the feud-hate into his heart.

The clamour of the central avenues drew him thitherward.   He had half expected to see Cal coming down the street in his shirtsleeves, with a jug and a whip in his hand, just as he would have seen him in Frankfort or Laurel City.   But an hour went by and Cal did not appear.   Perhaps he was waiting in ambush, to shoot him from a door or a window. Sam kept a sharp eye on doors and windows for a while.

About noon the city tired of playing with its mouse, and suddenly squeezed him with its straight lines.

Sam Folwell stood where two great, rectangular arteries of the city cross.   He looked four ways, and saw the world hurled from its orbit and reduced by spirit level and tape to an edged and cornered plane.   All life moved on tracks, in grooves, according to system, within boundaries, by rote.   The root of life was the cube root ;   the measure of existence was square   measure.   People   streamed   by   in straight rows ;   the horrible din and crash stupefied him.

Sam leaned against the sharp corner of a stone building.   Those faces passed him by thousands, and none of them were turned toward him.   A sudden foolish fear that he had died and was a spirit, and that they could not see him, seized him. And then the city smote him with loneliness.

A fat man dropped out of the stream and stood a few feet distant, waiting for his car. Sam crept to his side and shouted above the tumult into his ear:

"The Rankinses' hogs weighed more 'n ourn a whole passel, but the mast in thar neighbourhood was a fine chance better than what it was down ——"

The fat man moved away unostentatiously, and bought roasted chestnuts to cover his alarm.

Sam felt the need of a drop of mountain dew. Across the street men passed in and out through swinging doors. Brief glimpses could be had of a glistening bar and its bedeckings. The feudist crossed and essayed to enter. Again had Art eliminated the familiar circle. Sam's hand found no door-knob—it slid, in vain, over a rectangular brass plate and polished oak with nothing even so large as a pin's head upon which his fingers might close.

Abashed, reddened, heart-broken, he walked away from the bootless door and sat upon a step. A locust club tickled him in the ribs.

"Take a walk for yourself," said the policeman. "You 've been loafing around here long enough."

At the next corner a shrill whistle sounded in Sam's ear. He wheeled around and saw a black-browed villain scowling at him over peanuts heaped on a steaming machine. He started across the street. An immense engine, running without mules, with the voice of a bull and the smell of a smoky lamp, whizzed past, grazing his knee. A cab-driver bumped him with a hub, and explained to him that kind words were invented to be used on other occasions. A motorman clanged his bell wildly and, for once in his life, corroborated a cab-driver. A large lady in a changeable silk waist dug an elbow into his back, and a newsy pensively pelted him with banana rinds, murmuring, " I hates to do it—but if anybody seen me let it pass ! "

Cal Harkness, his day's work over and his express wagon stabled, turned the sharp edge of the building that, by the cheek of architects, is modelled upon a safety razor. Out of the mass of hurrying people his eye picked up, three yards away, the surviving bloody and implacable foe of his kith and kin.

He stopped short and wavered for a moment, being unarmed and sharply surprised. But the keen mountaineer's eye of Sam Folwell had picked him out.

There was a sudden spring, a ripple in the stream of passers-by, and the sound of Sam's voice crying :

" Howdy, Cal !   I 'm durned glad to see ye."

And in the angles of Broadway, Fifth Avenue and Twenty-third Street the Cumberland feudists shook hands.

ROSES, RUSES AND ROMANCE

RAVENEL—Ravenel, the traveller, artist and poet, threw his magazine to the floor. Sammy Brown, broker's clerk, who sat by the window, jumped.

" What is it, Ravvy ? " he asked. " The critics been hammering your stock down ? "

" Romance is dead," said Ravenel, lightly. When Ravenel spoke lightly he was generally serious. He picked up the magazine and fluttered its leaves.

" Even a Philistine, like you, Sammy," said Ravenel, seriously (a tone that insured him to be speaking lightly), " ought to understand. Now, here is a magazine that once printed Poe and Lowell and Whitman and Bret Harte and Du Maurier and Lanier and —well, that gives you the idea. The current number has this literary feast to set before you : an article on the stokers and coal bunkers of battleships, an exposé of the methods employed in making liverwurst, a continued story of a Standard Preferred International Baking Powder deal in Wall Street, a ' poem ' on the bear that the President missed, another ' story ' by a young woman who spent a week as a spy making overalls on the East Side, another ' fiction ' story that reeks of the ' garage ' and a certain make of automobile. Of course, the title contains the words ' Cupid' and ' Chauffeur '—an article on naval strategy illustrated with cuts of the Spanish Armada, and the new Staten Island ferry-boats ; another story of a political boss who won the love of a Fifth Avenue belle by blackening her eye and refusing to vote for an iniquitous ordinance (it doesn't say whether it was in the Street Cleaning Department or Congress), and nineteen pages by the editors bragging about the circulation. The whole thing, Sammy, is an obituary on Romance."

Sammy Brown sat comfortably in the leather arm-chair by the open window. His suit was a vehement brown with visible checks, beautifully matched in shade by the ends of four cigars that his vest pocket poorly concealed. Light tan were his shoes, grey his socks, sky-blue his apparent linen, snowy and high and adamantine his collar, against which a black butterfly had alighted and spread his wings. Sammy's face—least important—was round and pleasant and pinkish, and in his eyes you saw no haven for fleeing Romance.

That window of Ravenel's apartment opened upon an old garden full of ancient trees and shrubbery. The apartment-house towered above one side of it ; a high brick wall fended it from the street ; opposite Ravenel's window an old, old mansion stood, half-hidden in the shade of the summer foliage. The house was a castle besieged. The city howled and roared and shrieked and beat upon its double doors, and shook white, fluttering cheques above the wall, offering terms of surrender. The grey dust settled upon the trees; the siege was pressed hotter, but the drawbridge was not lowered. No further will the language of chivalry serve. Inside lived an old gentleman who loved his home and did not wish to sell it. That is all the romance of the besieged castle.

Three or four times every week came Sammy Brown to Ravenel's apartment. He belonged to the poet's club, for the former Browns had been conspicuous, though Sammy had been vulgarized by Business. He had no tears for departed Romance. The song of the ticker was the one that reached his heart, and when it came to matters equine and batting scores he was something of a pink edition. He loved to sit in the leather arm-chair by Ravenel's window. And Ravenel didn't mind particularly. Sammy seemed to enjoy his talk; and then the broker's clerk was such a perfect embodiment of modernity and the day's sordid practicality, that Ravenel rather liked to use him as a scapegoat.

" I 'll tell you what 's the matter with you," said Sammy, with the shrewdness that business had taught him. " The magazine has turned down some of your poetry stunts. That 's why you are sore at it."

" That would be a good guess in Wall Street
or in a campaign for the presidency of a woman's
club," said Ravenel, quietly. "Now, there
is a poem—if you will allow me to call it that
—of my own in this number of the magazine."

" Read it to me," said Sammy, watching a
cloud of pipe-smoke he had just blown out
the window.

Ravenel was no greater than Achilles. No
one is. There is bound to be a spot. The
Somebody-or-Other must take hold of us
somewhere when she dips us in the Something-
or-Other that makes us invulnerable, He read
aloud this verse in the magazine :

THE FOUR ROSES.

" One rose I twined within your hair—
    (White rose, that spake of worth) ;
And one you placed upon your breast—
    (Red rose, love's seal of birth).
You plucked another from its stem—
    (Tea rose, that means for aye) ;
And one you gave—that bore for me
    The thorns of memory."

" That 's a crackerjack," said Sammy,
admiringly.

" There are five more verses," said Ravenel,
patiently sardonic. "One naturally pauses
at the end of each. Of course —— "

" Oh, let 's have the rest, old man," shouted
Sammy, contritely, " I didn't mean to cut you
off. I 'm not much of a poetry expert, you
know. I never saw a poem that did'nt look

like it ought to have terminal facilities at the end of every verse. Reel off the rest of it."

Ravenel sighed, and laid the magazine down. "All right," said Sammy, cheerfully, "we'll have it next time. I'll be off now. Got a date at five o'clock."

He took a last look at the shaded green garden and left, whistling in an off key an untuneful air from a roofless farce comedy.

The next afternoon Ravenel, while polishing a ragged line of a new sonnet, reclined by the window overlooking the besieged garden of the unmercenary baron. Suddenly he sat up, spilling two rhymes and a syllable or two.

Through the trees one window of the old mansion could be seen clearly. In its window, draped in flowing white, leaned the angel of all his dreams of romance and poesy. Young, fresh as a drop of dew, graceful as a spray of clematis, conferring upon the garden hemmed in by the roaring traffic the air of a princess's bower, beautiful as any flower sung by poet— thus Ravenel saw her for the first time. She lingered for a while, and then disappeared within, leaving a few notes of a birdlike ripple of song to reach his entranced ears through the rattle of cabs and the snarling of the electric cars.

Thus, as if to challenge the poet's flaunt at romance and to punish him for his recreancy to the undying spirit of youth and beauty,

this vision had dawned upon him with a thrilling
and accusive power. And so metabolic was
the power, that in an instant the atoms of
Ravenel's entire world were redistributed.
The laden drays that passed the house in which
she lived rumbled a deep double-bass to the
tune of love. The newsboys' shouts were the
notes of singing birds ; that garden was the
pleasance of the Capulets ; the janitor was an
ogre ; himself a knight, ready with sword,
lance or lute.

Thus does romance show herself amid
forests of brick and stone when she gets lost in
the city, and there has to be sent out a general
alarm to find her again.

At four in the afternoon Ravenel looked
out across the garden. In the window of his
hopes were set four small vases, each containing
a great, full-blown rose—red and white. And,
as he gazed, she leaned above them, shaming
them with her loveliness and seeming to direct
her eyes pensively toward his own window.
And then, as though she had caught his
respectful but ardent regard, she melted
away, leaving the fragrant emblems on the
window-sill.

" Yes, emblems !—he would be unworthy
if he had not understood. She had read his
poem, " The Four Roses " ; it had reached
her heart ; and this was its romantic answer.
Of course, she must know that Ravenel, the
poet, lived across her garden. His picture, too,

she must have seen in the magazines. The delicate, tender, modest, flattering message could not be ignored.

Ravenel noticed beside the roses a small flowering-pot containing a plant. Without shame he brought his opera-glasses and employed them from the cover of his window-curtain. A nutmeg geranium!

With the true poetic instinct he dragged a book of useless information from his shelves, and tore open the leaves at " The Language of Flowers."

" Geranium, Nutmeg—I expect a meeting."

So! Romance never does things by halves. If she comes back to you she brings gifts and her knitting, and will sit in your chimney-corner if you will let her.

And now Ravenel smiled. The lover smiles when he thinks he has won. The woman who loves ceases to smile with victory. He ends a battle; she begins hers. What a pretty idea to set the four roses in her window for him to see! She must have a sweet, poetic soul. And now to contrive the meeting.

A whistling and slamming of doors preluded the coming of Sammy Brown.

Ravenel smiled again. Even Sammy Brown was shone upon by the far-flung rays of the renaissance. Sammy, with his ultra clothes, his horseshoe pin, his plump face, his trite slang, his uncomprehending admiration of Ravenel—the broker's clerk made an excellent foil to the new, bright, unseen visitor to the poet's sombre apartment.

Sammy went to his old seat by the window, and looked out over the dusty green foliage in the garden. Then he looked at his watch, and rose hastily.

" By grabs ! " he exclaimed. " Twenty after four ! I can't stay, old man ; I 've got a date at 4.30."

" Why did you come, then," asked Ravenel, with sarcastic jocularity, " if you had an engagement at that time ? I thought you business men kept better account of your minutes and seconds than that."

Sammy hesitated in the doorway and turned pinker.

" Fact is, Ravvy," he explained, as to a customer whose margin is exhausted, " I didn't know I had it till I came. I 'll tell you, old man—there 's a dandy girl in that old house next door that I 'm dead gone on. I put it straight—we 're engaged. The old man says ' nit '—but that don't go. He keeps her pretty close. I can see Edith's window from yours here. She gives me a tip when she 's going shopping, and I meet her. It 's 4.30 to-day. Maybe I ought to have explained sooner, but I know it 's all right with you—so long."

" How do you get your ' tip,' as you call it ? " asked Ravenel, losing a little spontaneity from his smile.

" Roses," said Sammy, briefly. " Four of

'em to-day. Means four o'clock at the corner of Broadway and Twenty-third."

"But the geranium?" persisted Ravenel, clutching at the end of flying Romance's trailing robe.

"Means half-past," shouted Sammy from the hall. "See you to-morrow."

THE CITY OF DREADFUL NIGHT

"DURING the recent warmed-over spell," said my friend Carney, driver of express wagon No. 8,606, "a good many opportunities was had of observing human nature through peekaboo waists.

"The Park Commissioner and the Commissioner of Polis and the Forestry Commission gets together and agrees to let the people sleep in the parks until the Weather Bureau gets the thermometer down again to a living basis. So they draws up open-air resolutions and has them O.K.'d by the Secretary of Agriculture, Mr. Comstock and the Village Improvement Mosquito Exterminating Society of South Orange, N.J.

"When the proclamation was made opening up to the people by special grant the public parks that belong to 'em, there was a general exodus into Central Park by the communities existing along its borders. In ten minutes after sundown you'd have thought that there was an undress rehearsal of a potato famine in Ireland and a Kishineff massacre. They come by families, gangs, clambake societies, clans, clubs and tribes from all sides to enjoy a cool sleep on the grass. Them that didn't have oil stoves brought along plenty of blankets, so as not to be upset with the cold and discomforts of sleeping outdoors. By building fires of the shade trees and huddling together in the bridle-paths, and burrowing under the grass where the ground was soft enough, the likes of 5,000 head of people successfully battled against the night air in Central Park alone.

" Ye know I live in the elegant furnished apartment house called the Beersheba Flats, over against the elevated portion of the New York Central Railroad.

" When the order come to the flats that all hands must turn out and sleep in the park, according to the instructions of the consulting committee of the City Club and the Murphy Draying, Returfing and Sodding Company, there was a look of a couple of fires and an eviction all over the place.

" The tenants began to pack up feather beds, rubber boots, strings of garlic, hot-water bags, portable canoes and scuttles of coal to take along for the sake of comfort. The sidewalk looked like a Russian camp in Oyama's line of march. There was wailing and lamenting up and down stairs from Danny Geoghegan's flat on the top floor to the apartments of Missis Goldsteinupski on the first.

" ' For why,' says Danny, coming down and raging in his blue yarn socks to the janitor, ' should I be turned out of me comfortable apartmints to lay in the dirty grass like a rabbit ? 'Tis like Jerome to stir up trouble wid small matters like this instead of —— "

" ' Whist ! ' says Officer Reagan on the sidewalk, rapping with his club. ' 'Tis not Jerome. 'Tis by order of the Polis Commissioner. Turn out every one of yez and hike yerselves to the park.'

" Now, 'twas a peaceful and happy home that all of us had in them same Beersheba Flats. The O'Dowds and the Steinowitzes and the Callahans and the Cohens and the Spizzinellis and the McManuses and the Spiegelmayers and the Joneses—all nations of us, we lived like one big family together. And when the hot nights come along we kept a line of childher reaching from the front door to Kelly's on the corner, passing along the cans of beer from one to another without the trouble of running after it. And with no more clothing on than is provided for in the statutes, sitting in all the windies, with a cool growler in every one, and your feet out in the air, and the Rosenstein girls singing on the fire-escape of the sixth floor, and Patsy Rourke's flute going in the eighth, and the ladies calling each other synonyms out the windies, and now and then a breeze sailing in over Mister Depew's Central —I tell you the Beersheba Flats was a summer resort that made the Catskills look like a hole in the ground. With his person full of beer and his feet out the windy and his old woman frying pork chops over a charcoal furnace, and the childher dancing in cotton slips on the sidewalk around the organ-grinder and the rent paid for a week—what does a man want better on a hot night than that? And then comes this ruling of the polis driving people out o' their comfortable homes to sleep in parks—'twas for all the world like a ukase of them Russians—'twill be heard from again at next election time.

"Well, then, Officer Reagan drives the whole lot of us to the park and turns us in by the nearest gate. 'Tis dark under the trees, and all the childher sets up to howling that they want to go home.

"'Ye'll pass the night in this stretch of woods and scenery,' says Officer Reagan. ''Twill be fine and imprisonment for insoolting the Park Commissioner and the Chief of the Weather Bureau if ye refuse. I'm in charge of thirty acres between here and the Agyptian Monument, and I advise ye to give no trouble. 'Tis sleeping on the grass yez all have been condemned to by the authorities. Yez'll be permitted to leave in the morning, but ye must retoorn be night. Me orders was silent on the subject of bail, but I'll find out if 'tis required and there'll be bondsmen at the gate.'

"There being no lights except al-ng the automobile drives, us 179 tenants of the Beersheba Flats prepared to spend the night as best we could in the raging forest. Them that brought blankets and kindling wood was best off. They got fires started and wrapped the blankets round their heads and laid down, cursing, in the grass. There was nothing to see, nothing to drink, nothing to do. In the dark we had no way of telling friend or foe except by feeling the noses of 'em. I brought along me last winter overcoat, me tooth-brush, some quinine pills, and the red quilt off the bed in me flat. Three times during the night somebody rolled on me quilt and stuck his knees against the Adam's apple of me. And three times I judged his character by running me hand over his face, and three times I rose up and kicked the intruder down the hill to the gravelly walk below. And then someone with a flavour of Kelly's whisky snuggled up to me, and I found his nose turned up the right way, and I says : ' Is that you, then, Patsey ? ' and he says, ' It is, Carney. How long do you think it 'll last ? '

" ' I 'm no weather-prophet,' says I, ' but if they bring out a strong anti-Tammany ticket next fall it ought to get us home in time to sleep on a bed once or twice before they line us up at the polls.'

" ' A-playing of my flute into the airshaft,' says Patsey Rourke, ' and a-perspiring in me own windy to the joyful noise of the passing trains and the smell of liver and onions and a-reading of the latest murder in the smoke of the cooking is well enough for me,' says he. ' What is this herding us in grass for, not to mention the crawling things with legs that walk up the trousers of us, and the Jersey snipes that peck at us, masquerading under the name and denomination of mosquitoes? What is it all for, Carney, and the rint going on just the same over at the flats?'

" ' 'Tis the great annual Municipal Free Night Outing Lawn Party,' says I, ' given by the polis, Hetty Green, and the Drug Trust. During the heated season they hold a week of it in the principal parks. 'Tis a scheme to reach that portion of the people that's not worth taking up to North Beach for a fish fry.'

" ' I can't sleep on the ground,' says Patsey, ' wid any benefit. I have the hay fever and the rheumatism, and me ear is full of ants.'

" Well, the night goes on, and the ex-tenants of the Flats groans and stumbles around in the dark, trying to find rest and recreation in the forest. The childher is screaming with the coldness, and the janitor makes hot tea for 'em, and keeps the fires going with the signboards that point to the Tavern and the Casino. The tenants try to lay down on the grass by families in the dark, but you 're lucky if you can sleep next to a man from the same floor or believing in the same religion. Now and then a Murphy, accidental, rolls over on the grass of a Rosenstein, or a Cohen tries to crawl under the O'Grady bush, and then there's a feeling of noses, and somebody is rolled down the hill to the driveway and stays there. There is some hair-pulling among the women folks, and everybody spanks the nearest howling kid to him by the sense of feeling only, regardless of its parentage and ownership. 'Tis hard to keep up the social distinctions in the dark that flourish by daylight in the Beersheba Flats. Mrs. Rafferty, that despises the asphalt that a Dago treads on, wakes up in the morning with her feet in the bosom of Antonio Spizzinelli. And Mike O'Dowd, that always threw peddlers downstairs as fast as he came upon 'em, has to unwind old Isaacstein's whiskers from around his neck, and wake up the whole gang at daylight. But here and there some few got acquainted and overlooked the discomforts of the elements. There was five engagements to be married announced at the flats the next morning.

"About midnight I gets up and wrings the dew out of my hair, and goes to the side of the driveway and sits down. At one side of the park I could see the lights in the streets and houses ; and I was thinking how happy them folks was who could chase the duck and smoke their pipes at their windows, and keep cool and pleasant like Nature intended for 'em to.

"Just then an automobile stops by me, and a fine-looking, well-dressed man steps out.

"'Me man,' says he, 'can you tell me why all these people are lying around on the grass in the park ? I thought it was against the rules.'

" ' 'Twas an ordinance,' says I, ' just passed by the Polis Department and ratified by the Turf Cutters' Association, providing that all persons not carrying a licence number on their rear axles shall keep in the public parks until further notice. Fortunately, the orders comes this year during a spell of fine weather, and the mortality, except on the borders of the lake and along the automobile drives, will not be any greater than usual.'

" ' Who are these people on the side of the hill ? ' asks the man.

" ' Sure,' says I, ' none others than the tenants of the Beersheba Flats—a fine home for any man, especially on hot nights. May daylight come soon ! '

" ' They come here be night,' says he, ' and breathe in the pure air and the fragrance of the flowers and trees. They do that,' says he, ' coming every night from the burning heat of dwellings of brick and stone.'

" ' And wood,' says I. ' And marble and plaster and iron.'

" ' The matter will be attended to at once,' says the man, putting up his book.

" ' Are ye the Park Commissioner ? ' I asks.

" ' I own the Beersheba Flats,' says he. ' God bless the grass and the trees that give extra benefits to a man's tenants. The rents shall be raised fifteen per cent. to-morrow. Good night,' says he."

THE EASTER OF THE SOUL

IT is hardly likely that a goddess may die.
Then Eastre, the old Saxon goddess of spring,
must be laughing in her muslin sleeve at people
who believe that Easter, her namesake, exists
only along certain strips of Fifth Avenue pavement after church service.

Aye! It belongs to the world. The
ptarmigan in Chilkoot Pass discards his winter
white feathers for brown; the Patagonian
Beau Brummell oils his chignon and clubs him
another sweetheart to drag to his skull-strewn
flat. And down in Chrystie Street——

Mr. "Tiger" McQuirk arose with a feeling
of disquiet that he did not understand. With a
practised foot he rolled three of his younger
brothers like logs out of his way as they lay
sleeping on the floor. Before a foot-square
looking-glass hung by the window he stood and
shaved himself. If that may seem to you a
task too slight to be thus impressively chronicled
I bear with you; you do not know of the areas
to be accomplished in traversing the cheek and
chin of Mr. McQuirk.

McQuirk, senior, had gone to work long
before. The big son of the house was idle. He
was a marble-cutter, and the marble-cutters
were out on a strike.

" What ails ye ? " asked his mother, looking at him curiously ; " are ye not feeling well the morning, maybe now ? "

" He 's thinking along of Annie Maria Doyle," impudently explained younger brother Tim, ten years old.

" Tiger " reached over the hand of a champion and swept the small McQuirk from his chair.

" I feel fine," said he, " beyond a touch of the I-don't-know-what-you-call-its. I feel like there was going to be earthquakes or music or a trifle of chills and fever or maybe a picnic. I don't know how I feel. I feel like knocking the face off a policeman, or else maybe like playing Coney Island straight across the board from pop-corn to the elephant houdahs."

" It 's the spring in yer bones," said Mrs. McQuirk. " It 's the sap risin'. Time was when I couldn't keep me feet still nor me head cool when the earthworms began to crawl out in the dew of the mornin'. 'Tis a bit of tea will do ye good, made from pipsissewa and gentian bark at the druggist's."

" Back up ! " said Mr. McQuirk, impatiently. " There 's no spring in sight. There 's snow yet on the shed in Donovan's backyard. And yesterday they puts open cars on the Sixth Avenue lines, and the janitors have quit ordering coal. And that means six weeks more of winter, by all the signs that be."

After breakfast Mr. McQuirk spent fifteen

minutes before the corrugated mirror, subjuga-
ting his hair and arranging his green-and-purple
ascot with its amethyst tombstone pin—
eloquent of his chosen calling.

Since the strike had been called it was this
particular striker's habit to hie himself each
morning to the corner saloon of Flaherty
Brothers, and there establish himself upon the
sidewalk, with one foot resting on the bootblack's stand, observing the panorama of the
street until the pace of time brought twelve
o'clock and the dinner hour. And Mr. " Tiger "
McQuirk, with his athletic seventy inches,
well trained in sport and battle, his smooth,
pale, solid, amiable face—blue where the razor
had travelled, his carefully-considered clothes
and air of capability, was himself a spectacle
not displeasing to the eye.

But on this morning Mr. McQuirk did not
hasten immediately to his post of leisure and
observation. Something unusual that he could
not quite grasp was in the air. Something
disturbed his thoughts, ruffled his senses, made
him at once languid, irritable, elated,
dissatisfied and sportive. He was no
diagnostician, and he did not know that Lent
was breaking up physiologically in his system.

Mrs. McQuirk had spoken of spring.
Sceptically " Tiger " looked about him for
signs. Few they were. The organ-grinders
were at work ; but they were always precocious
harbingers. It was near enough spring for

them to go penny-hunting when the skating ball dropped at the park. In the milliners' windows Easter hats, grave, gay and jubilant, blossomed. There were green patches among the sidewalk debris of the grocers. On a third-story window-sill the first elbow cushion of the season—old gold stripes on a crimson ground—supported the kimonoed arms of a pensive brunette. The wind blew cold from the East River, but the sparrows were flying to the eaves with straws. A second-hand store, combining foresight with faith, had set out an ice-chest and baseball goods.

And then " Tiger's " eye, discrediting these signs, fell upon one that bore a bud of promise. From a bright, new lithograph the head of Capricornus confronted him, betokening the forward and heady brew.

Mr. McQuirk entered the saloon and called for his glass of bock. He threw his nickel on the bar, raised the glass, set it down without tasting it, and strolled toward the door.

" Wot 's the matter, Lord Bolinbroke ? " inquired the sarcastic bar-tender ; " want a chiny vase or a gold-lined epergne to drink it out of—hey ? "

" Say," said Mr. McQuirk, wheeling and shooting out a horizontal hand and a forty-five-degree chin, " you know your place only when it comes for givin' titles. I 've changed me mind about drinkin'—see ? You got your money, ain't you ? Wait till you get stung before you get the droop to your lip, will you ? "

Thus Mr. McQuirk added mutability of desires to the strange humours that had taken possession of him.

Leaving the saloon, he walked away twenty steps, and leaned in the open doorway of Lutz, the barber. He and Lutz were friends, masking their sentiments behind abuse and bludgeons of repartee.

" Irish loafer," roared Lutz, " how do you do ? So, not yet haf der bolicemans or der catcher of dogs done deir duty ! "

" Hello, Dutch," said Mr. McQuirk. " Can't get your mind off of frankfurters, can you ? "

" Bah ! " exclaimed the German, coming and leaning in the doorway. " I haf a soul above frankfurters to-day. Dere is springtime in der air. I can feel it coming in ofer der mud of der streets and das ice in der river. Soon will dere be bicnics in der islands, mit kegs of beer under der trees."

" Say," said Mr. McQuirk, setting his hat on one side, " is everybody kiddin' me about gentle Spring ? There ain't any more spring in the air than there is in a horsehair sofa in a Second Avenue furnished room. For me the winter underwear yet and the buckwheat cakes."

" You haf no boetry," said Lutz. " True, it is yedt cold, und in der city we haf not many of der signs ; but dere are dree kinds of beoble dot should always feel der approach of

6

spring first—dey are boets, lovers and poor vidows."

Mr. McQuirk went on his way, still possessed by the strange perturbation that he did not understand. Something was lacking to his comfort, and it made him half angry because he did not know what it was.

Two blocks away he came upon a foe, one Conover, whom he was bound in honour to engage in combat.

Mr. McQuirk made the attack with the characteristic suddenness and fierceness that had gained for him the endearing sobriquet of "Tiger." The defence of Mr. Conover was so prompt and admirable that the conflict was protracted, until the onlookers unselfishly gave the warning cry of "Cheese it—the cop!" The principals escaped easily by running through the nearest open doors into the communicating backyards at the rear of the houses.

Mr. McQuirk emerged into another street. He stood by a lamp-post for a few minutes engaged in thought, and then he turned and plunged into a small notion and news shop. A red-haired young woman, eating gum-drops, came and looked freezingly at him across the ice-bound steppes of the counter.

"Say, lady," he said, "have you got a song book with this in it. Let 's see how it leads off—

" When the springtime comes we 'll wander in the dale, love,
    And whisper of those days of yore —— "

"I'm having a friend," explained Mr. McQuirk, "laid up with a broken leg, and he sent me after it. He's a devil for songs and poetry when he can't get out to drink."

"We have not," replied the young woman, with unconcealed contempt. "But there is a new song out that begins this way :

"'Let us sit together in the old arm-chair ;
    And while the firelight flickers we'll be comfortable
        there.'"

There will be no profit in following Mr. "Tiger" McQuirk through his further vagaries of that day until he comes to stand knocking at the door of Annie Maria Doyle. The goddess Eastre, it seems, had guided his footsteps aright at last.

"Is that you now, Jimmy McQuirk ?" she cried, smiling through the opened door (Annie Maria had never accepted the "Tiger"). "Well, whatever !"

"Come out in the hall," said Mr. McQuirk. "I want to ask yer opinion of the weather—on the level."

"Are you crazy, sure ?" said Annie Maria.

"I am," said the "Tiger." "They've been telling me all day there was spring in the air. Were they liars ? Or am I ?"

"Dear me !" said Annie Maria—"haven't you noticed it ? I can almost smell the violets. And the green grass. Of course, there ain't any yet—it's just a kind of feeling, you know."

"That's what I'm getting at," said

Mr. McQuirk. "I've had it. I didn't recognize it at first. I thought maybe it was en-wee, contracted the other day when I stepped above Fourteenth Street. But the katzenjammer I've got don't spell violets. It spells yer own name, Annie Maria, and it's you I want. I go to work next Monday, and I make four dollars a day. Spiel up, old girl—do we make a team?"

"Jimmy," sighed Annie Maria, suddenly disappearing in his overcoat, "don't you see that spring is all over the world right this minute?"

But you yourself remember how that day ended. Beginning with so fine a promise of vernal things, late in the afternoon the air chilled and an inch of snow fell—even so late in March. On Fifth Avenue the ladies drew their winter furs close about them. Only in the florists' windows could be perceived any signs of the morning smile of the coming goddess Eastre.

At six o'clock Herr Lutz began to close his shop. He heard a well-known shout: "Hello, Dutch!"

"Tiger" McQuirk, in his shirt-sleeves, with his hat on the back of his head, stood outside in the whirling snow, puffing at a black cigar.

"Donnerwetter!" shouted Lutz, "der vinter, he has gome back again yet!"

"Yer a liar, Dutch," called back Mr. McQuirk, with friendly geniality, "it's springtime, by the watch."

THE FOOL-KILLER

DOWN South whenever anyone perpetrates some particularly monumental piece of foolishness everybody says : " Send for Jesse Holmes."

Jesse Holmes is the Fool-Killer. Of course he is a myth, like Santa Claus and Jack Frost and General Prosperity and all those concrete conceptions that are supposed to represent an idea that Nature has failed to embody. The wisest of the Southrons cannot tell you whence comes the Fool-Killer's name ; but few and happy are the households from the Roanoke to the Rio Grande in which the name of Jesse Holmes has not been pronounced or invoked. Always with a smile, and often with a tear, is he summoned to his official duty. A busy man is Jesse Holmes.

I remember the clear picture of him that hung on the walls of my fancy during my barefoot days when I was dodging his oft-threatened devoirs. To me he was a terrible old man, in grey clothes, with a long, ragged, grey beard, and reddish, fierce eyes. I looked to see him come stumping up the road in a cloud of dust, with a white oak staff in his hand and his shoes tied with leather thongs. I may yet——

But this is a story, not a sequel.

I have taken notice with regret, that few stories worth reading have been written that did not contain drink of some sort. Down go the fluids, from Arizona Dick's three fingers of red pizen to the inefficacious Oolong that nerves Lionel Montressor to repartee in the "Dotty Dialogues." So, in such good company I may introduce an absinthe drip — one absinthe drip, dripped through a silver dripper, orderly, opalescent, cool, green-eyed — deceptive.

Kerner was a fool. Besides that, he was an artist and my good friend. Now, if there is one thing on earth utterly despicable to another, it is an artist in the eyes of an author whose story he has illustrated. Just try it once. Write a story about a mining camp in Idaho. Sell it. Spend the money, and then, six months later, borrow a quarter (or a dime), and buy the magazine containing it. You find a full-page wash drawing of your hero, Black Bill, the cowboy. Somewhere in your story you employed the word "horse." Aha! the artist has grasped the idea. Black Bill has on the regulation trousers of the M. F. H. of the Westchester County Hunt. He carries a parlour rifle, and wears a monocle. In the distance is a section of Forty-second Street during a search for a lost gas-pipe, and the Taj Mahal, the famous mausoleum in India.

Enough ! I hated Kerner, and one day I met him, and we became friends. He was young and gloriously melancholy because his spirits were so high and life had so much in store for him. Yes, he was almost riotously sad. That was his youth. When a man begins to be hilarious in a sorrowful way you can bet a million that he is dyeing his hair. Kerner's hair was plentiful, and carefully matted as an artist's thatch should be. He was a cigaretteur, and he audited his dinners with red wine. But, most of all, he was a fool. And, wisely, I envied him, and listened patiently while he knocked Velasquez and Tintoretto. Once he told me that he liked a story of mine that he had come across in an anthology. He described it to me, and I was sorry that Mr. FitzJames O'Brien was dead and could not learn of the eulogy of his work. But mostly Kerner made few breaks and was a consistent fool.

I 'd better explain what I mean by that. There was a girl. Now, a girl, as far as I am concerned, is a thing that belongs in a seminary or an album ; but I conceded the existence of the animal in order to retain Kerner's friendship. He showed me her picture in a locket—she was a blonde or a brunette—I have forgotten which. She worked in a factory for eight dollars a week. Lest factories quote this wage by way of vindication, I will add that the girl had worked for five years to reach that supreme elevation of remuneration, beginning at $1.50 per week.

Kerner's father was worth a couple of millions. He was willing to stand for art, but he drew the line at the factory girl. So Kerner disinherited his father, and walked out to a cheap studio, and lived on sausages for breakfast and on Farroni for dinner. Farroni had the artistic soul and a line of credit for painters and poets, nicely adjusted. Sometimes Kerner sold a picture and bought some new tapestry, a ring and a dozen silk cravats, and paid Farroni two dollars on account.

One evening Kerner had me to dinner with himself and the factory girl. They were to be married as soon as Kerner could slosh paint profitably. As for the ex-father's two millions —pouf !

She was a wonder. Small and half-way pretty, and as much at her ease in that cheap café as though she were only in the Palmer House, Chicago, with a souvenir spoon already safely hidden in her shirt waist. She was natural. Two things I noticed about her especially. Her belt buckle was exactly in the middle of her back, and she didn't tell us that a large man with a ruby stick-pin had followed her up all the way from Fourteenth Street. Was Kerner such a fool? I wondered. And then I thought of the quantity of striped cuffs and blue glass beads that $2,000,000 can buy for the heathen, and I said to myself

that he was. And then Elise—certainly that
was her name—told us, merrily, that the brown
spot on her waist was caused by her landlady
knocking at the door while she (the girl—
confound the English language) was heating an
iron over the gas-jet, and she hid the iron under
the bedclothes until the coast was clear, and
there was the piece of chewing gum stuck to it
when she began to iron the waist, and—well, I
wondered how in the world the chewing
gum came to be there—don't they ever stop
chewing it ?

A while after that—don't be impatient, the
absinthe drip is coming now—Kerner and I
were dining at Farroni's. A mandolin and a
guitar were being attacked ; the room was
full of smoke in nice, long, crinkly layers
just like the artists draw the steam from a
plum pudding on Christmas posters, and a
lady in a blue silk and gasolined gauntlets
was beginning to hum an air from the
Catskills.

" Kerner," said I, " you are a fool."

" Of course," said Kerner, " I wouldn't let
her go on working. Not my wife. What 's
the use to wait ? She 's willing. I sold that
water-colour of the Palisades yesterday. We
could cook on a two-burner gas stove. You
know the ragouts I can throw together ? Yes,
I think we will marry next week."

" Kerner," said I, " you are a fool."

" Have an absinthe drip ? " said Kerner,

6 *

grandly. "To-night you are the guest of Art
in paying quantities. I think we will get a
flat with a bath."

"I never tried one—I mean an absinthe
drip," said I.

The waiter brought it and poured the water
slowly over the ice in the dripper.

"It looks exactly like the Mississippi River
water in the big bend below Natchez,"
said I, fascinated, gazing at the be-muddled
drip.

"There are such flats for eight dollars a
week," said Kerner.

"You are a fool," said I, and began to sip
the filtration. "What you need," I continued, "is the official attention of one Jesse
Holmes."

Kerner, not being a Southerner, did not
comprehend, so he sat, sentimental, figuring
on his flat in his sordid, artistic way, while I
gazed into the green eyes of the sophisticated
Spirit of Wormwood.

Presently I noticed casually that a procession
of bacchantes limned on the wall immediately
below the ceiling had begun to move, traversing
the room from right to left in a gay and
spectacular pilgrimage. I did not confide my
discovery to Kerner. The artistic temperament is too high-strung to view such deviations
from the natural laws of the art of kalsomining.
I sipped my absinthe drip and sawed wormwood.

One absinthe drip is not much—but I said again to Kerner, kindly :

" You are a fool." And then, in the vernacular : " Jesse Holmes for yours."

And then I looked around and saw the Fool-Killer, as he had always appeared to my imagination, sitting at a nearby table, and regarding us with his reddish, fatal, relentless eyes. He was Jesse Holmes from top to toe ; he had the long, grey, ragged beard, the grey clothes of ancient cut, the executioner's look, and the dusty shoes of one who had been called from afar. His eyes were turned fixedly upon Kerner. I shuddered to think that I had invoked him from his assiduous southern duties. I thought of flying, and then I kept my seat, reflecting that many men had escaped his ministrations when it seemed that nothing short of an appointment as Ambassador to Spain could save them from him. I had called my brother Kerner a fool, and was in danger of hell fire. That was nothing ; but I would try to save him from Jesse Holmes.

The Fool-Killer got up from his table and came over to ours. He rested his hands upon it, and turned his burning, vindictive eyes upon Kerner, ignoring me.

" You are a hopeless fool," he said to the artist. " Haven't you had enough of starvation yet ? I offer you one more opportunity. Give up this girl and come back to your home. Refuse, and you must take the consequences."

The Fool-Killer's threatening face was within a foot of his victim's; but, to my horror, Kerner made not the slightest sign of being aware of his presence.

" We will be married next week," he muttered absent-mindedly. " With my studio furniture and some second-hand stuff we can make out."

" You have decided your own fate," said the Fool-Killer, in a low but terrible voice. " You may consider yourself as one dead. You have had your last chance."

" In the moonlight," went on Kerner, softly, " we will sit under the skylight with our guitar and sing away the false delights of pride and money."

" On your own head be it," hissed the Fool-Killer, and my scalp prickled when I perceived that neither Kerner's eyes nor his ears took the slightest cognizance of Jesse Holmes. And then I knew that for some reason the veil had been lifted for me alone, and that I had been elected to save my friend from destruction at the Fool-Killer's hands. Something of the fear and wonder of it must have showed itself in my face.

" Excuse me," said Kerner, with his wan, amiable smile ; " was I talking to myself ? I think it is getting to be a habit with me."

The Fool-Killer turned and walked out of Farroni's.

" Wait here for me," said I, rising ; " I must

speak to that man. Had you no answer for him ? Because you are a fool must you die like a mouse under his foot ? Could you not utter one squeak in your own defence ? "

" You are drunk," said Kerner, heartlessly. " No one addressed me."

" The destroyer of your mind," said I, " stood above you just now and marked you for his victim. You are not blind or deaf."

" I recognized no such person," said Kerner. " I have seen no one but you at this table. Sit down. Hereafter you shall have no more absinthe drips."

" Wait here," said I, furious ; " if you don't care for your own life, I will save it for you."

I hurried out and overtook the man in grey half-way down the block. He looked as I had seen him in my fancy a thousand times— truculent, grey and awful. He walked with the white oak staff, and but for the street-sprinkler the dust would have been flying under his tread.

I caught him by the sleeve and steered him to a dark angle of a building. I knew he was a myth, and I did not want a cop to see me conversing with vacancy, for I might land in Bellevue minus my silver matchbox and diamond ring.

" Jesse Holmes," said I, facing him with apparent bravery, " I know you. I have heard of you all my life. I know now what a scourge

you have been to your country. Instead of
killing fools you have been murdering the
youth and genius that are necessary to make a
people live and grow great. You are a fool
yourself, Holmes; you began killing off the
brightest and best of your countrymen three
generations ago, when the old and obsolete
standards of society and honour and orthodoxy
were narrow and bigoted. You proved that
when you put your murderous mark upon my
friend Kerner—the wisest chap I ever knew
in my life."

The Fool-Killer looked at me grimly and
closely.

"You've a queer jag," said he, curiously.
"Oh, yes; I see who you are now. You were
sitting with him at the table. Well, if I'm
not mistaken, I heard you call him a fool, too."

"I did," said I. "I delight in doing so.
It is from envy. By all the standards that you
know he is the most egregious and grandiloquent
and gorgeous fool in all the world. That's
why you want to kill him."

"Would you mind telling me who or what
you think I am?" asked the old man.

I laughed boisterously and then stopped
suddenly, for I remembered that it would not
do to be seen so hilarious in the company of
nothing but a brick wall.

"You are Jesse Holmes, the Fool-Killer,"
I said, solemnly, "and you are going to kill
my friend Kerner. I don't know who rang

you up, but if you do kill him I 'll see that you
get pinched for it. That is," I added,
despairingly, " if I can get a cop to see you.
They have a poor eye for mortals, and I think
it would take the whole force to round up a
myth murderer."

" Well," said the Fool-Killer, briskly, " I
must be going. You had better go home
and sleep it off. Good night."

At this I was moved by a sudden fear for
Kerner to a softer and more pleading mood.
I leaned against the grey man's sleeve and
besought him :

" Good Mr. Fool-Killer, please don't kill
little Kerner. Why can't you go back South
and kill Congressmen and clay-eaters and let
us alone ? Why don't you go up on Fifth
Avenue and kill millionaires, that keep their
money locked up, and won't let young fools
marry because one of 'em lives on the wrong
street ? Come and have a drink, Jesse. Will
you never get on to your job ? "

" Do you know this girl that your friend has
made himself a fool about ? " asked the
Fool-Killer.

" I have the honour," said I, " and that 's
why I called Kerner a fool. He is a fool because
he has waited so long before marrying her. He
is a fool because he has been waiting in the
hopes of getting the consent of some absurd
two-million-dollar-fool parent or something
of the sort."

"Maybe," said, the Fool-Killer—"maybe I—I might have looked at it differently. Would you mind going back to the restaurant and bringing your friend Kerner here?"

"Oh, what's the use, Jesse," I yawned. "He can't see you. He didn't know you were talking to him at the table. You are a fictitious character, you know."

"Maybe he can this time. Will you go fetch him?"

"All right," said I, "but I've a suspicion that you're not strictly sober, Jesse. You seem to be wavering and losing your outlines. Don't vanish before I get back."

I went back to Kerner and said:

"There's a man with an invisible homicidal mania waiting to see you outside. I believe he wants to murder you. Come along. You won't see him, so there's nothing to be frightened about."

Kerner looked anxious.

"Why," said he, "I had no idea one absinthe would do that. You'd better stick to Würzburger. I'll walk home with you."

I led him to Jesse Holmes's.

"Rudolf," said the Fool-Killer, "I'll give in. Bring her up to the house. Give me your hand, boy."

"Good for you, dad," said Kerner, shaking hands with the old man. "You'll never regret it after you know her."

"So, you did see him when he was talking to you at the table?" I asked Kerner.

"We hadn't spoken to each other in a year," said Kerner. "It's all right now."

I walked away.

"Where are you going?" called Kerner.

"I am going to look for Jesse Holmes," I answered, with dignity and reserve.

THERE is a hotel on Broadway that has escaped discovery by the summer-resort promoters. It is deep and wide and cool. Its rooms are finished in dark oak of a low temperature. Home-made breezes and deep-green shrubbery give it the delights without the inconveniences of the Adirondacks. One can mount its broad staircases or glide dreamily upward in its aerial elevators, attended by guides in brass buttons, with a serene joy that Alpine climbers have never attained. There is a chef in its kitchen who will prepare for you brook trout better than the White Mountains ever served, sea food that would turn Old Point Comfort—" by Gad, sah ! "—green with envy, and Maine venison that would melt the official heart of a game warden.

A few have found out this oasis in the July desert of Manhattan. During that month you will see the hotel's reduced array of guests scattered luxuriously about in the cool twilight of its lofty dining-room, gazing at one another across the snowy waste of unoccupied tables, silently congratulatory.

Superfluous, watchful, pneumatically moving waiters hover near, supplying every want before it is expressed. The temperature is perpetual

April. The ceiling is painted in water-colours to counterfeit a summer sky across which delicate clouds drift and do not vanish as those of Nature do to our regret.

The pleasing, distant roar of Broadway is transformed in the imagination of the happy guests to the noise of a waterfall filling the woods with its restful sound.   At every strange footstep the guests turn an anxious ear, fearful lest their retreat be discovered and invaded by the restless pleasure-seekers who are for ever hounding Nature to her deepest lairs

Thus in the depopulated caravansary the little band of connoisseurs jealously hide themselves during the heated season, enjoying to the uttermost the delights of mountain and seashore that art and skill have gathered and served to them.

In this July came to the hotel one whose card that she sent to the clerk for her name to be registered read " Mme. Héloise D'Arcy Beaumont."

Madame Beaumont was a guest such as the Hotel Lotus loved. She possessed the fine air of the élite, tempered and sweetened by a cordial graciousness that made the hotel employés her slaves.   Bell-boys fought for the honour of answering her ring ; the clerks, but for the question of ownership, would have deeded to her the hotel and its contents ; the other guests regarded her as the final touch of feminine exclusiveness and beauty that rendered the entourage perfect.

This super-excellent guest rarely left the hotel. Her habits were consonant with the customs of the discriminating patrons of the Hotel Lotus. To enjoy that delectable hostelry one must forego the city as though it were leagues away. By night a brief excursion to the nearby roofs is in order ; but during the torrid day one remains in the umbrageous fastnesses of the Lotus as a trout hangs poised in the pellucid sanctuaries of his favourite pool.

Though alone in the Hotel Lotus, Madame Beaumont preserved the state of a queen whose loneliness was of position only. She breakfasted at ten, a cool, sweet, leisurely, delicate being who glowed softly in the dimness like a jasmine flower in the dusk.

But at dinner was Madame's glory at its height. She wore a gown as beautiful and immaterial as the mist from an unseen cataract in a mountain gorge. The nomenclature of this gown is beyond the guess of the scribe. Always pale-red roses reposed against its lace-garnished front. It was a gown that the head waiter viewed with respect and met at the door. You thought of Paris when you saw it, and maybe of mysterious countesses, and certainly of Versailles and rapiers and Mrs. Fiske and rouge-et-noir. There was an untraceable rumour in the Hotel Lotus that Madame was a cosmopolite, and that she was pulling

with her slender white hands certain strings
between the nations in the favour of Russia.
Being a citizeness of the world's smoothest
roads, it was small wonder that she was quick
to recognize in the refined purlieus of the Hotel
Lotus the most desirable spot in America for
a restful sojourn during the heat of midsummer.

On the third day of Madame Beaumont's
residence in the hotel a young man entered
and registered himself as a guest. His clothing
—to speak of his points in approved order—
was quietly in the mode ; his features good
and regular ; his expression that of a poised
and sophisticated man of the world. He
informed the clerk that he would remain three
or four days, inquired concerning the sailing of
European steamships, and sank into the blissful
inanition of the nonpareil hotel with the
contented air of a traveller in his favourite inn.

The young man—not to question the veracity
of the register—was Harold Farrington. He
drifted into the exclusive and calm current of
life in the Lotus so tactfully and silently that
not a ripple alarmed his fellow-seekers after
rest. He ate in the Lotus and of its patronym,
and was lulled into blissful peace with the other
fortunate mariners. In one day he acquired
his table and his waiter and the fear lest the
panting chasers after repose that kept Broadway
warm should pounce upon and destroy this
contiguous but covert haven.

After dinner on the next day after the arrival

of Harold Farrington Madame Beaumont
dropped her handkerchief in passing out. Mr.
Farrington recovered and returned it without
the effusiveness of a seeker after acquaintance.

Perhaps there was a mystic freemasonry
between the discriminating guests of the Lotus.
Perhaps they were drawn one to another by
the fact of their common good fortune in
discovering the acme of summer resorts in
a Broadway hotel. Words delicate in courtesy
and tentative in departure from formality
passed between the two. And, as if in the
expedient atmosphere of a real summer resort,
an acquaintance grew, flowered, and fructified
on the spot as does the mystic plant of the
conjuror. For a few moments they stood on
a balcony upon which the corridor ended, and
tossed the feathery ball of conversation.

" One tires of the old resorts," said Madame
Beaumont, with a faint but sweet smile. " What
is the use to fly to the mountains or the seashore
to escape noise and dust when the very people
that make both follow us there ? "

" Even on the ocean," remarked Farrington,
sadly, " the Philistines be upon you. The most
exclusive steamers are getting to be scarcely
more than ferry-boats. Heaven help us when
the summer resorter discovers that the Lotus
is farther away from Broadway than Thousand
Islands or Mackinac."

" I hope our secret will be safe for a week,
anyhow," said Madame, with a sigh and a smile.

" I do not know where I would go if they should descend upon the dear Lotus. I know of but one place so delightful in summer, and that is the castle of Count Polinski, in the Ural Mountains."

" I hear that Baden-Baden and Cannes are almost deserted this season," said Farrington. " Year by year the old resorts fall in disrepute. Perhaps many others, like ourselves, are seeking out the quiet nooks that are overlooked by the majority."

" I promise myself three days more of this delicious rest," said Madame Beaumont. " On Monday the *Cedric* sails."

Harold Farrington's eyes proclaimed his regret. " I too must leave on Monday," he said, " but I do not go abroad."

Madame Beaumont shrugged one round shoulder in a foreign gesture.

" One cannot hide here for ever, charming though it may be. The château has been in preparation for me longer than a month. Those house parties that one must give—what a nuisance ! But I shall never forget my week in the Hotel Lotus."

" Nor shall I," said Farrington in a low voice, " and I shall never *forgive* the *Cedric*."

On Sunday evening, three days afterward, the two sat at a little table on the same balcony. A discreet waiter brought ices and small glasses of claret cup.

Madame Beaumont wore the same beautiful

evening gown that she had worn each day at
dinner. She seemed thoughtful. Near her
hand on the table lay a small chatelaine purse.
After she had eaten her ice she opened the
purse and took out a one-dollar bill.

"Mr. Farrington," she said, with the smile
that had won the Hotel Lotus, "I want to tell
you something. I'm going to leave before
breakfast in the morning, because I've got to
go back to my work. I'm behind the hosiery
counter at Casey's Mammoth Store, and my
vacation's up at eight o'clock to-morrow. That
paper dollar is the last cent I'll see till I draw
my eight dollars salary next Saturday night.
You're a real gentleman, and you've been
good to me, and I wanted to tell you before I
went.

"I've been saving up out of my wages for
a year just for this vacation. I wanted to
spend one week like a lady if I never do another
one. I wanted to get up when I please instead
of having to crawl out at seven every morning ;
and I wanted to live on the best and be waited
on and ring bells for things just like rich folks
do. Now, I've done it, and I've had the
happiest time I ever expect to have in my life.
I'm going back to my work and my little hall
bedroom satisfied for another year. I wanted
to tell you about it, Mr. Farrington, because
I—I thought you kind of liked me, and I—I
liked you. But, oh, I couldn't help deceiving
you up till now, for it was all just like a fairy

tale to me.   So I talked about Europe and the things I've read about in other countries, and made you think I was a great lady.

" This dress I've got on—it's the only one I have that's fit to wear—I bought from O'Dowd & Levinsky on the instalment plan.

" Seventy-five dollars is the price, and it was made to measure. I paid $10 down, and they're to collect $1 a week till it's paid for.   That'll be about all I have to say, Mr. Farrington, except that my name is Mamie Siviter instead of Madame Beaumont, and I thank you for your attentions.   This dollar will pay the instalment due on the dress to-morrow.   I guess I'll go up to my room now."

Harold Farrington listened to the recital of the Lotus's loveliest guest with an impassive countenance.   When she had concluded he drew a small book like a cheque-book from his coat pocket.   He wrote upon a blank form in this with a stub of pencil, tore out the leaf, tossed it over to his companion, and took up the paper dollar.

" I've got to go to work, too, in the morning," he said, " and I might as well begin now. There's a receipt for the dollar instalment. I've been a collector for O'Dowd & Levinsky for three years.   Funny, ain't it, that you and me both had the same idea about spending our vacation ?   I've always wanted to put up at a swell hotel, and I saved up out of my

twenty per, and did it.   Say, Mamie, how about
a trip to Coney Saturday night on the boat—
what ? "

The face of the pseudo Madame Héloise
D'Arcy Beaumont beamed.

" Oh, you bet I 'll go, Mr. Farrington.   The
store closes at twelve on Saturdays.   I guess
Coney 'll be all right even if we did spend a
week with the swells."

Below the balcony the sweltering city
growled and buzzed in the July night.   Inside
the Hotel Lotus the tempered, cool shadows
reigned, and the solicitous waiter single-footed
near the low windows, ready at a nod to serve
Madame and her escort.

At the door of the elevator Farrington took
his leave, and Madame Beaumont made her
last ascent.   But before they reached the
noiseless cage he said : " Just forget that
' Harold Farrington,' will you ?—McManus is
the name—James McManus.   Some call me
Jimmy."

" Good night, Jimmy," said Madame.

THE RATHSKELLER AND THE ROSE

Miss Posie Carrington had earned her success. She began life handicapped by the family name of " Boggs," in the small town known as Cranberry Corners. At the age of eighteen she had acquired the name of " Carrington " and a position in the chorus of a metropolitan burlesque company. Thence upward she had ascended by the legitimate and delectable steps of " broiler," member of the famous " Dickey-bird " octette, in the successful musical comedy, " Fudge and Fellows," leader of the potato-bug dance in " Fol-de-Rol," and at length to the part of the maid " 'Toinette " in " The King's Bath-Robe," which captured the critics and gave her her chance. And when we come to consider Miss Carrington she is in the hey-day of flattery, fame, and fizz ; and that astute manager, Herr Timothy Goldstein, has her signature to iron-clad papers that she will star the coming season in Dyde Rich's new play, " Paresis by Gaslight."

Promptly there came to Herr Timothy a capable twentieth-century young character actor by the name of Highsmith, who besought engagement as " Sol Haytosser," the comic and chief male character part in " Paresis by Gaslight."

"My boy," said Goldstein, "take the part if you can get it. Miss Carrington won't listen to any of my suggestions. She has turned down half a dozen of the best imitators of the rural dub in the city. She declares she won't set a foot on the stage unless 'Haytosser' is the best that can be raked up. She was raised in a village, you know, and when a Broadway orchid sticks a straw in his hair and tries to call himself a clover blossom she's on, all right. I asked her, in a sarcastic vein, if she thought Denman Thompson would make any kind of a show in the part. 'Oh, no,' says she. 'I don't want him or John Drew or Jim Corbett, or any of these swell actors that don't know a turnip from a turnstile. I want the real article.' So, my boy, if you want to play 'Sol Haytosser' you will have to convince Miss Carrington. Luck be with you."

Highsmith took the train the next day for Cranberry Corners. He remained in that forsaken and inanimate village three days. He found the Boggs family and corkscrewed their history unto the third and fourth generation. He amassed the facts and the local colour of Cranberry Corners. The village had not grown as rapidly as had Miss Carrington. The actor estimated that it had suffered as few actual changes since the departure of its solitary follower of Thespis as had a stage upon which "four years is supposed to have elapsed."

He absorbed Cranberry Corners and returned to the city of chameleon changes.

It was in the rathskeller that Highsmith made the hit of his histrionic career. There is no need to name the place ; there is but one rathskeller where you could hope to find Miss Posie Carrington after a performance of " The King's Bath-Robe."

There was a jolly small party at one of the tables that drew many eyes. Miss Carrington, petite, marvellous, bubbling, electric, fame-drunken, shall be named first. Herr Goldstein follows, sonorous, curly-haired, heavy, a trifle anxious, as some bear that had caught, some-how, a butterfly in his claws. Next, a man condemned to a newspaper, sad, courted, armed, analyzing for press agent's dross every sentence that was poured over him, eating his à la Newburg in the silence of greatness. To conclude, a youth with parted hair, a name that is ochre to red journals and gold on the back of a supper cheque. These sat at a table while the musicians played, while waiters moved in the mazy performance of their duties with their backs toward all who desired their service, and all was bizarre and merry because it was nine feet below the level of the sidewalk.

At 11.45 a being entered the rathskeller. The first violin perceptibly flatted a C that should have been natural, the clarionet blew a bubble instead of a grace note, Miss Carrington giggled, and the youth with parted hair swallowed an olive seed.

Exquisitely and irreproachably rural was the new entry. A lank, disconcerted, hesitating young man it was, flaxen-haired, gaping of mouth, awkward, stricken to misery by the lights and company. His clothing was butternut, with bright blue tie, showing four inches of bony wrist and white-socked ankle. He upset a chair, sat in another one, curled a foot around a table leg, and cringed at the approach of a waiter.

"You may fetch me a glass of lager beer," he said, in response to the discreet questioning of the servitor.

The eyes of the rathskeller were upon him. He was as fresh as a collard and as ingenuous as a hayrake. He let his eye rove about the place as one who regards, big-eyed, hogs in the potato patch. His gaze rested at length upon Miss Carrington. He rose and went to her table with a lateral, shining smile and a blush of pleased trepidation.

"How 're ye, Miss Posie?" he said in accents not to be doubted. "Don't ye remember me—Bill Summers—the Summerses that lived back of the blacksmith shop? I reckon I 've growed up some since ye left Cranberry Corners.

"'Liza Perry 'lowed I might see ye in the city while I was here. You know 'Liza married Benny Stanfield, and she says ——"

"Ah, say!" interrupted Miss Carrington, brightly, "Lize Perry is never married—what! Oh, the freckles of her!"

"Married in June," grinned the gossip, "and livin' in the old Tatum Place. Ham Riley perfessed religion; old Mrs. Blithers sold her place to Cap'n Spooner; the youngest Waters girl run away with a music teacher; the court-house burned up last March; your Uncle Wiley was elected constable; Matilda Hoskins died from runnin' a needle in her hand; and Tom Beedle is courtin' Sallie Lathrop—they say he don't miss a night but what he's settin' on their porch."

"The wall-eyed thing!" exclaimed Miss Carrington, with asperity. "Why, Tom Beedle once—say, you folks, excuse me a while—this is an old friend of mine—Mr.—what was it? Yes, Mr. Summers—Mr. Goldstein, Mr. Ricketts, Mr.——. Oh, what's yours? 'Johnny' 'll do—come on over here and tell me some more."

She swept him to an isolated table in a corner. Herr Goldstein shrugged his fat shoulders and beckoned to the waiter. The newspaper man brightened a little and mentioned absinthe. The youth with parted hair was plunged into melancholy. The guests of the rathskeller laughed, clinked glasses, and enjoyed the comedy that Posie Carrington was treating them to after her regular performance. A few cynical ones whispered "press agent" and smiled wisely.

Posie Carrington laid her dimpled and desirable chin upon her hands, and forgot her audience—a faculty that had won her laurels for her.

" I don't seem to recollect any Bill Summers," she said, thoughtfully gazing straight into the innocent blue eyes of the rustic young man. " But I know the Summerses, all right. I guess there ain't many changes in the old town. You see any of my folks lately ? "

And then Highsmith played his trump. The part of " Sol Haytosser " called for pathos as well as comedy. Miss Carrington should see that he could do that as well.

" Miss Posie," said " Bill Summers," " I was up to your folkeses house jist two or three days ago. No, there ain't many changes to speak of. The lilac bush by the kitchen window is over a foot higher, and the elm in the front yard died and had to be cut down. And yet it don't seem the same place that it used to be."

" How 's ma ? " asked Miss Carrington.

" She was settin' by the front door, crocheting a lamp-mat when I saw her last," said " Bill." " She 's older 'n she was, Miss Posie. But everything in the house looked jest the same. Your ma asked me to set down. ' Don't touch that willow rocker, William,' says she. ' It ain't been moved since Posie left ; and that 's the apron she was hemmin', layin' over the arm of it, jist as she flung it. I 'm in hopes,' she goes on, ' that Posie 'll finish runnin' out that hem some day.' "

Miss Carrington beckoned peremptorily to a waiter.

" A pint of extra dry," she ordered, briefly ; " and give the check to Goldstein."

" The sun was shinin' in the door," went on the chronicler from Cranberry, " and your ma was settin' right in it. I asked her if she hadn't better move back a little. ' William,' says she, ' when I get sot down and lookin' down the road, I can't bear to move. Never a day,' says she, ' but what I set here every minute that I can spare and watch over them palin's for Posie. She went away down that road in the night, for we seen her little shoe tracks in the dust, and somethin' tells me she 'll come back that way ag'in when she 's weary of the world and begins to think about her old mother.'

" When I was comin' away," concluded " Bill," " I pulled this off 'n the bush by the front steps. I thought maybe I might see you in the city, and I knowed you 'd like somethin' from the old home."

He took from his coat pocket a rose—a drooping, yellow, velvet, odorous rose, that hung its head in the foul atmosphere of that tainted rathskeller like a virgin bowing before the hot breath of the lions in a Roman arena.

Miss Carrington's penetrating but musical laugh rose above the orchestra's rendering of " Bluebells."

7

"Oh, say!" she cried, with glee, "ain't those poky places the limit? I just know that two hours at Cranberry Corners would give me the horrors now. Well, I'm awful glad to have seen you, Mr. Summers. I guess I'll hustle around to the hotel now and get my beauty sleep."

She thrust the yellow rose into the bosom of her wonderful, dainty, silken garments, stood up, and nodded imperiously at Herr Goldstein.

Her three companions and "Bill Summers" attended her to her cab. When her flounces and streamers were all safely tucked inside she dazzled them with au revoirs from her shining eyes and teeth.

"Come around to the hotel and see me, Bill, before you leave the city," she called as the glittering cab rolled away.

Highsmith, still in his make-up, went with Herr Goldstein to a café booth.

"Bright idea, eh?" asked the smiling actor. "Ought to land 'Sol Haytosser' for me, don't you think? The little lady never once tumbled."

"I didn't hear your conversation," said Goldstein, "but your make-up and acting was O. K. Here's to your success. You'd better call on Miss Carrington early to-morrow and strike her for the part. I don't see how she can keep from being satisfied with your exhibition of ability."

At 11.45 a.m. on the next day Highsmith, handsome, dressed in the latest mode, confident, with a fuchsia in his button-hole, sent up his card to Miss Carrington in her select apartment hotel.

He was shown up and received by the actress's French maid.

" I am sorree," said Mlle. Hortense, " but I am to say this to all. It is with great regret. Mees Carrington have cancelled all engagements on the stage, and have returned to live in that —how you call that town ? Cranberry Cornaire ! "

THE CLARION CALL

HALF of this story can be found in the records of the Police Department; the other half belongs behind the business counter of a newspaper office.

One afternoon two weeks after Millionaire Norcross was found in his apartment murdered by a burglar, the murderer, while strolling serenely down Broadway, ran plump against Detective Barney Woods.

"Is that you, Johnny Kernan?" asked Woods, who had been near-sighted in public for five years.

"No less," cried Kernan, heartily. "If it isn't Barney Woods, late and early of old Saint Jo! You'll have to show me! What are you doing East? Do the green-goods circulars get out that far?"

"I've been in New York some years," said Woods. "I'm on the city detective force."

"Well, well!" said Kernan, breathing smiling joy and patting the detective's arm.

"Come into Muller's," said Woods, "and let's hunt a quiet table. I'd like to talk to you awhile."

It lacked a few minutes to the hour of four. The tides of trade were not yet loosed, and they found a quiet corner of the café. Kernan, well dressed, slightly swaggering, self-confident, seated himself opposite the little detective, with his pale, sandy moustache, squinting eyes, and ready-made cheviot suit.

"What business are you in now?" asked Woods. "You know you left Saint Jo a year before I did."

"I'm selling shares in a copper mine," said Kernan. "I may establish an office here. Well, well! and so old Barney is a New York detective. You always had a turn that way. You were on the police in Saint Jo after I left there, weren't you?"

"Six months," said Woods. "And now there's one more question, Johnny. I've followed your record pretty close ever since you did that hotel job in Saratoga, and I never knew you to use your gun before. Why did you kill Norcross?"

Kernan stared for a few moments with concentrated attention at the slice of lemon in his high-ball; and then he looked at the detective with a sudden, crooked, brilliant smile.

"How did you guess it, Barney?" he asked, admiringly. "I swear I thought the job was as clean and as smooth as a peeled onion. Did I leave a string hanging out anywhere?"

Woods laid upon the table a small gold pencil intended for a watch-charm.

"It's the one I gave you the last Christmas we were in Saint Jo. I've got your shaving

mug yet. I found this under a corner of the
rug in Norcross's room. I warn you to be
careful what you say. I 've got it put on to
you, Johnny. We were old friends once, but
I must do my duty. You 'll have to go to
the chair for Norcross."

Kernan laughed.

" My luck stays with me," said he. " Who 'd
have thought old Barney was on my trail ! "
He slipped one hand inside his coat. In an
instant Woods had a revolver against his side.

" Put it away," said Kernan, wrinkling his
nose. " I 'm only investigating. Aha ! It
takes nine tailors to make a man, but one can
do a man up. There 's a hole in that vest
pocket. I took that pencil off my chain and
slipped it in there in case of a scrap. Put
up your gun, Barney, and I 'll tell you why I
had to shoot Norcross. The old fool started
down the hall after me, popping at the buttons
on the back of my coat with a peevish little
.22, and I had to stop him. The old lady was
a darling. She just lay in bed and saw her
$12,000 diamond necklace go without a chirp,
while she begged like a panhandler to have back
a little thin gold ring with a garnet worth
about $3. I guess she married old Norcross
for his money, all right. Don't they hang on
to the little trinkets from the Man Who Lost
Out, though ? There were six rings, two
brooches, and a chatelaine watch. Fifteen
thousand would cover the lot."

"I warned you not to talk," said Woods.

"Oh, that's all right," said Kernan. "The stuff is in my suit-case at the hotel. And now I'll tell you why I'm talking. Because it's safe. I'm talking to a man I know. You owe me a thousand dollars, Barney Woods, and even if you wanted to arrest me your hand wouldn't make the move."

"I haven't forgotten," said Woods. "You counted out twenty fifties without a word. I'll pay it back some day. That thousand saved me, and—well, they were piling my furniture out on the sidewalk when I got back to the house."

"And so," continued Kernan, "you being Barney Woods, born as true as steel, and bound to play a white man's game, can't lift a finger to arrest the man you're indebted to. Oh, I have to study men as well as Yale locks and window fastenings in my business. Now, keep quiet while I ring for the waiter. I've had a thirst for a year or two that worries me a little. If I'm ever caught, the lucky sleuth will have to divide honours with old boy Booze. But I never drink during business hours. After a job I can crook elbows with my old friend Barney with a clear conscience. What are you taking?"

The waiter came with the little decanters and the siphon and left them alone again.

"You've called the turn," said Woods, as he rolled the little gold pencil about with a thoughtful forefinger. " I 've got to pass you up. I can't lay a hand on you. If I 'd a-paid that money back—but I didn't, and that settles it. It 's a bad break I 'm making, Johnny, but I can't dodge it. You helped me once, and it calls for the same."

" I knew it," said Kernan, raising his glass, with a flushed smile of self-appreciation. " I can judge men. Here 's to Barney, for—' he 's a jolly good fellow.' "

" I don't believe," went on Woods quietly, as if he were thinking aloud, " that if accounts had been square between you and me, all the money in all the banks in New York could have bought you out of my hands to-night."

" I know it couldn't," said Kernan. " That 's why I knew I was safe with you."

" Most people," continued the detective, " look sideways at my business. They don't class it among the fine arts and the professions. But I 've always taken a kind of fool pride in it. And here is where I go ' busted.' I guess I 'm a man first and a detective afterward. I 've got to let you go, and then I 've got to resign from the force. I guess I can drive an express wagon. Your thousand dollars is farther off than ever, Johnny."

" Oh, you 're welcome to it," said Kernan, with a lordly air. " I 'd be willing to call the debt off, but I know you wouldn't have it. It was a lucky day for me when you borrowed it. And now, let 's drop the subject. I 'm

off to the West on a morning train. I know a
place out there where I can negotiate the
Norcross sparks. Drink up, Barney, and forget
your troubles. We 'll have a jolly time while
the police are knocking their heads together
over the case. I 've got one of my Sahara
thirsts on to-night. But I 'm in the hands—
the unofficial hands—of my old friend Barney,
and I won't even dream of a cop."

And then, as Kernan's ready finger kept the
button and the waiter working, his weak
point—a tremendous vanity and arrogant
egotism—began to show itself. He recounted
story after story of his successful plunderings,
ingenious plots and infamous transgressions
until Woods, with all his familiarity with evil-
doers, felt growing within him a cold abhorrence
toward the utterly vicious man who had once
been his benefactor.

"I 'm disposed of, of course," said Woods,
at length. "But I advise you to keep under
cover for a spell. The newspapers may take
up this Norcross affair. There has been an
epidemic of burglaries and manslaughter in
town this summer."

The word sent Kernan into a high glow of
sullen and vindictive rage.

"To h—l with the newspapers," he
growled. "What do they spell but brag and
blow and boodle in box-car letters? Suppose
they do take up a case—what does it amount
to? The police are easy enough to fool;

but what do the newspapers do ? They send
a lot of pin-head reporters around to the scene ;
and they make for the nearest saloon and have
beer, while they take photos of the bar-tender's
oldest daughter in evening dress, to print as
the fiancée of the young man in the tenth story,
who thought he heard a noise below on the
night of the murder. That 's about as near as
the newspapers ever come to running down
Mr. Burglar."

" Well, I don't know," said Woods, reflecting.
" Some of the papers have done good work in
that line. There 's the *Morning Mars*, for
instance. It warmed up two or three trails,
and got the man after the police had let 'em
get cold."

" I 'll show you," said Kernan, rising, and
expanding his chest. " I 'll show you what I
think of newspapers in general, and your
Morning Mars in particular."

Three feet from their table was the telephone
booth. Kernan went inside and sat at the
instrument, leaving the door open. He found
a number in the book, took down the receiver,
and made his demand upon Central. Woods
sat still, looking at the sneering, cold, vigilant
face waiting close to the transmitter, and
listened to the words that came from the
thin, truculent lips curved into a contemptuous
smile.

" That the *Morning Mars ?* . . . I want
to speak to the managing editor . . . Why,

tell him it's someone who wants to talk to him about the Norcross murder.

"You the editor? . . . All right. . . . I am the man who killed old Norcross. . . . Wait! Hold the wire; I'm not the usual crank. . . . Oh, there isn't the slightest danger. I've just been discussing it with a detective friend of mine. I killed the old man at 2.30 a.m. two weeks ago to-morrow. . . . Have a drink with you? Now, hadn't you better leave that kind of talk to your funny man? Can't you tell whether a man's guying you or whether you're being offered the biggest scoop your dull dish-rag of a paper ever had? . . . Well, that's so; it's a bobtail scoop—but you can hardly expect me to 'phone in my name and address. . . . Why? Oh, because I heard you make a speciality of solving mysterious crimes that stump the police. . . . No, that's not all. I want to tell you that your rotten, lying, penny sheet is of no more use in tracking an intelligent murderer or highwayman than a blind poodle would be. . . . What? . . . Oh, no, this isn't a rival newspaper office; you're getting it straight. I did the Norcross job, and I've got the jewels in my suit-case at —'the name of the hotel could not be learned'—you recognize that phrase, don't you? I thought so. You've used it often enough. Kind of rattles you, doesn't it, to have the mysterious villain call up your great, big, all-powerful organ of right and justice and good government and tell you what a helpless old gas-bag you are ?   . . .   Cut that out ; you're not that big a fool—no, you don't think I'm a fraud. I can tell it by your voice. . . . Now, listen, and I'll give you a pointer that will prove it to you. Of course, you've had this murder case worked over by your staff of bright young blockheads. Half of the second button on old Mrs. Norcross's nightgown is broken off. I saw it when I took the garnet ring off her finger. I thought it was a ruby. . . . Stop that ! it won't work."

Kernan turned to Woods with a diabolic smile.

" I 've got him going. He believes me now. He didn't quite cover the transmitter with his hand when he told somebody to call up Central on another 'phone and get our number. I'll give him just one more dig, and then we'll make a ' get-away.'

" Hello ! . . . Yes. I 'm here yet. You didn't think I 'd run from such a little subsidized turn-coat rag of a newspaper, did you ? . . . Have me inside of forty-eight hours ? Say, will you quit being funny ? Now, you let grown men alone, and attend to your business of hunting up divorce cases and street-car accidents, and printing the filth and scandal that you make your living by. Good-bye, old boy— sorry I haven't time to call on you. I 'd feel perfectly safe in your sanctum asinorum. Tra-la ! "

" He 's as mad as a cat that 's lost a mouse,"
said Kernan, hanging up the receiver and
coming out. "And now, Barney, my boy,
we 'll go to a show and enjoy ourselves until
a reasonable bedtime. Four hours' sleep for
me, and then the west-bound."

The two dined in a Broadway restaurant.
Kernan was pleased with himself. He spent
money like a prince of fiction. And then a
weird and gorgeous musical comedy engaged
their attention. Afterward there was a late
supper in a grillroom, with champagne, and
Kernan at the height of his complacency.

Half-past three in the morning found them
in a corner of an all-night café, Kernan still
boasting in a vapid and rambling way, Woods
thinking moodily over the end that had come
to his usefulness as an upholder of the law.

But, as he pondered, his eye brightened with
a speculative light.

" I wonder if it 's possible," he said to himself,
" I won-der if it 's pos-si-ble ! "

And then outside the café the comparative
stillness of the early morning was punctured by
faint, uncertain cries that seemed mere fireflies
of sound, some growing louder, some fainter,
waxing and waning amid the rumble of milk-
wagons and infrequent cars. Shrill cries they
were when near—well-known cries that conveyed
many meanings to the ears of those of the
slumbering millions of the great city who waked
to hear them. Cries that bore upon their

significant, small volume the weight of a world's woe and laughter and delight and stress. To some, cowering beneath the protection of a night's ephemeral cover, they brought news of the hideous, bright day ; to others, wrapped in happy sleep, they announced a morning that would dawn blacker than sable night. To many of the rich they brought a besom to sweep away what had been theirs while the stars shone ; to the poor they brought— another day.

All over the city the cries were starting up, keen and sonorous, heralding the chances that the slipping of one cogwheel in the machinery of time had made ; apportioning to the sleepers while they lay at the mercy of fate the vengeance, profit, grief, reward, and doom that the new figure in the calendar had brought them. Shrill and yet plaintive were the cries, as if the young voices grieved that so much evil and so little good was in their irresponsible hands. Thus echoed in the streets of the helpless city the transmission of the latest decrees of the gods, the cries of the newsboys—the Clarion Call of the Press.

Woods flipped a dime to the waiter, and said :

" Get me a *Morning Mars*."

When the paper came he glanced at its first page, and then tore a leaf out of his memorandum book and began to write on it with the little gold pencil.

" What 's the news ? " yawned Kernan.

Woods flipped over to him the piece of writing :

" The New York *Morning Mars :*

" Please pay to the order of John Kernan the one thousand dollars reward coming to me for his arrest and conviction.

" BARNARD WOODS."

" I kind of thought they would do that," said Woods, " when you were jollying 'em so hard. Now, Johnny, you 'll come to the police station with me."

EXTRADITED FROM BOHEMIA

FROM near the village of Harmony, at the foot of the Green Mountains, came Miss Medora Martin to New York with her colour-box and easel.

Miss Medora resembled the rose which the autumnal frosts had spared the longest of all her sister blossoms. In Harmony, when she started alone to the wicked city to study art, they said she was a mad, reckless, headstrong girl. In New York, when she first took her seat at a West Side boarding-house table, the boarders asked: "Who is the nice-looking old maid?"

Medora took heart, a cheap hall bedroom, and two art lessons a week from Professor Angelini, a retired barber who had studied his profession in a Harlem dancing academy. There was no one to set her right, for here in the big city they do it unto all of us. How many of us are badly shaved daily and taught the two-step imperfectly by ex-pupils of Bastien Le Page and Gérôme? The most pathetic sight in New York—except the manners of the rush-hour crowds—is the dreary march of the hopeless army of Mediocrity. Here Art is no benignant goddess, but a Circe who turns her wooers into mewing Toms and Tabbies who

204

linger about the doorsteps of her abode, unmindful of the flying brickbats and boot-jacks of the critics. Some of us creep back to our native villages to the skim-milk of " I told you so " ; but most of us prefer to remain in the cold courtyard of our mistress's temple, snatching the scraps that fall from her divine table d'hôte. But some of us grow weary at last of the fruitless service. And then there are two fates open to us. We can get a job driving a grocer's wagon, or we can get swallowed up in the Vortex of Bohemia. The latter sounds good ; but the former really pans out better. For when the grocer pays us off we can rent a dress-suit and—the capitalized system of humour describes it best—Get Bohemia On the Run.

Miss Medora chose the Vortex, and thereby furnishes us with our little story.

Professor Angelini praised her sketches excessively. Once when she had made a neat study of a horse-chestnut tree in the park he declared she would become a second Rosa Bonheur. Again—a great artist has his moods — he would say cruel and cutting things. For example, Medora had spent an afternoon patiently sketching the statue and the architecture at Columbus Circle. Tossing it aside with a sneer, the professor informed her that Giotto had once drawn a perfect circle with one sweep of his hand.

One day it rained, the weekly remittance from Harmony was overdue, Medora had a headache,

the professor had tried to borrow two dollars
from her, her art dealer had sent back all her
water-colours unsold, and—Mr. Binkley asked
her out to dinner.

Mr. Binkley was the gay boy of the boarding-
house. He was forty-nine, and owned a fish-stall
in a down-town market. But after six o'clock
he wore an evening suit and whooped things
up connected with the beaux arts. The young
men said he was an "Indian." He was
supposed to be an accomplished habitué of
the inner circles of Bohemia. It was no
secret that he had once loaned $10 to a young
man who had had a drawing printed in *Puck*.
Often has one thus obtained his entrée into the
charmed circle, while the other obtained both
his entrée and roast.

The other boarders enviously regarded
Medora as she left at Mr. Binkley's side at
nine o'clock. She was as sweet as a cluster
of dried autumn grasses in her pale blue—oh
—er—that very thin stuff—in her pale blue
Comstockized silk waist and box-pleated voile
skirt, with a soft pink glow on her thin cheeks
and the tiniest bit of rouge powder on her
face, with her handkerchief and room key in
her brown walrus, pebble-grain hand-bag.

And Mr. Binkley looked imposing and dashing
with his red face and grey moustache, and his
tight dress-coat, that made the back of his neck
roll up just like a successful novelist's.

They drove in a cab to the Café Terence

just off the most glittering part of Broadway,
which, as everyone knows, is one of the most
popular and widely - patronized, jealously
exclusive Bohemian resorts in the city.

Down between the rows of little tables
tripped Medora, of the Green Mountains, after
her escort. Thrice in a lifetime may woman
walk upon clouds—once when she trippeth to
the altar, once when she first enters Bohemian
halls, the last when she marches back across
her first garden with the dead hen of her
neighbour in her hand.

There was a table set, with three or four
about it. A waiter buzzed around it like a
bee, and silver and glass shone upon it. And,
preliminary to the meal, as the prehistoric
granite strata heralded the protozoa, the bread
of Gaul, compounded after the formula of the
recipe for the eternal hills, was there set forth
to the hand and tooth of a long-suffering city,
while the gods lay beside their nectar and
home - made biscuits and smiled, and the
dentists leaped for joy in their gold-leafy dens.

The eye of Binkley fixed a young man at
his table with the Bohemian gleam, which is
a compound of the look of the Basilisk, the shine
of a bubble of Würzburger, the inspiration of
genius, and the pleading of a panhandler.

The young man sprang to his feet. " Hello,
Bink, old boy ! " he shouted. " Don't tell
me you were going to pass our table. Join
us—unless you 've another crowd on hand."

"Don't mind, old chap," said Binkley, of the fish-stall. "You know how I like to butt up against the fine arts. Mr. Vandyke —Mr. Madder— er —Miss Martin, one of the elect also in art—er —— "

The introduction went around. There were also Miss Elise and Miss 'Toinette. Perhaps they were models, for they chattered of the St. Regis decorations and Henry James—and they did it not badly.

Medora sat in transport. Music—wild, intoxicating music made by troubadours direct from a rear basement room in Elysium—set her thoughts to dancing. Here was a world never before penetrated by her warmest imagination or any of the lines controlled by Harriman. With the Green Mountains' external calm upon her she sat, her soul flaming in her with the fire of Andalusia. The tables were filled with Bohemia. The room was full of the fragrance of flowers—both mille and cauli. Questions and corks popped ; laughter and silver rang ; champagne flashed in the pail, wit flashed in the pan.

Vandyke ruffled his long, black locks, disarranged his careless tie, and leaned over to Madder.

"Say, Maddy," he whispered, feelingly, "sometimes I 'm tempted to pay this Philistine his ten dollars and get rid of him."

Madder ruffled his long, sandy locks and disarranged his careless tie.

"Don't think of it, Vandy," he replied.
"We are short, and Art is long."

Medora ate strange viands and drank
elderberry wine that they poured in her glass.
It was just the colour of that in the Vermont
home. The waiter poured something in another
glass that seemed to be boiling, but when she
tasted it it was not hot. She had never felt
so light-hearted before. She thought lovingly
of the Green Mountain farm and its fauna.
She leaned, smiling, to Miss Elise.

"If I were at home," she said, beamingly,
"I could show you the cutest little calf!"

"Nothing for you in the White Lane," said
Miss Elise. "Why don't you pad?"

The orchestra played a wailing waltz that
Medora had learned from the hand-organs.
She followed the air with nodding head in a
sweet soprano hum. Madder looked across
the table at her, and wondered in what strange
waters Binkley had caught her in his seine.
She smiled at him, and they raised glasses and
drank of the wine that boiled when it was cold.
Binkley had abandoned art, and was prating of
the unusual spring catch of shad. Miss Elise
arranged the palette-and-maul-stick tie-pin of
Mr. Vandyke. A Philistine at some distant
table was maundering volubly either about
Jerome or Gérôme. A famous actress was
discoursing excitably about monogrammed
hosiery. A hose clerk from a department
store was loudly proclaiming his opinions of

the drama. A writer was abusing Dickens.
A magazine editor and a photographer were
drinking a dry brand at a reserved table. A
36-25-42 young lady was saying to an eminent
sculptor : " Fudge for your Prax Italys !
Bring one of your Venus Anno Dominis down
to Cohen's and see how quick she 'd be turned
down for a cloak model. Back to the quarries
with your Greeks and Dagos ! "

Thus went Bohemia.

At eleven Mr. Binkley took Medora to the
boarding-house and left her, with a society bow,
at the foot of the hall stairs. She went up to
her room and lit the gas.

And then, as suddenly as the dreadful genie
arose in vapour from the copper vase of the
fisherman, arose in that room the formidable
shape of the New England Conscience. The
terrible thing that Medora had done was
revealed to her in its full enormity. She had
sat in the presence of the ungodly, and
looked upon the wine both when it was red and
effervescent.

At midnight she wrote this letter .

" MR. BERIAH HOSKINS, Harmony, Vermont.

" Dear Sir,—Henceforth consider me as
dead to you for ever. I have loved you too
well to blight your career by bringing into it
my guilty and sin-stained life. I have
succumbed to the insidious wiles of this wicked
world, and have been drawn into the Vortex of

Bohemia. There is scarcely any depth of glittering iniquity that I have not sounded. It is hopeless to combat my decision. There is no rising from the depths to which I have sunk. Endeavour to forget me. I am lost for ever in the fair but brutal maze of awful Bohemia. Farewell.

"ONCE YOUR MEDORA."

On the next day Medora formed her resolutions. Beelzebub, flung from heaven, was no more cast down. Between her and the apple blossoms of Harmony there was a fixed gulf. Flaming cherubim warded her from the gates of her lost paradise. In one evening, by the aid of Binkley and Mumm, Bohemia had gathered her into its awful midst.

There remained to her but one thing—a life of brilliant but irremediable error. Vermont was a shrine that she never would dare to approach again. But she would not sink—there were great and compelling ones in history upon whom she would model her meteoric career—Camille, Lola Montez, Royal Mary, Zaza—such a name as one of these would that of Medora Martin be to future generations.

For two days Medora kept her room. On the third she opened a magazine at the portrait of the King of Belgium, and laughed sardonically. If that far-famed breaker of women's hearts should cross her path, he would have to bow before her cold and imperious beauty. She would not spare the old or the young. All America—all Europe should do homage to her sinister but compelling charm.

As yet she could not bear to think of the life she had once desired—a peaceful one in the shadow of the Green Mountains with Beriah at her side, and orders for expensive oil paintings coming in by each mail from New York. Her one fatal misstep had shattered that dream.

On the fourth day Medora powdered her face and rouged her lips. Once she had seen Carter in " Zaza." She stood before the mirror in a reckless attitude and cried : " Zut ! zut ! " She rhymed it with " nut," but with the lawless word Harmony seemed to pass away for ever. The Vortex had her. She belonged to Bohemia for evermore And never would Beriah ——

The door opened and Beriah walked in.

" 'Dory," said he, " what 's all that chalk and pink stuff on your face, honey ? "

Medora extended an arm.

" Too late," she said, solemnly. " The die is cast. I belong in another world. Curse me if you will—it is your right. Go, and leave me in the path I have chosen. Bid them all at home never to mention my name again. And sometimes, Beriah, pray for me when I am revelling in the gaudy but hollow, pleasures of Bohemia."

" Get a towel, 'Dory," said Beriah, " and wipe that paint off your face. I came as soon as I got your letter. Them pictures of yours ain't amounting to anything. I 've got tickets for both of us back on the evening train. Hurry and get your things in your trunk."

" Fate was too strong for me, Beriah. Go while I am strong to bear it."

" How do you fold this easel, 'Dory ?—now begin to pack, so we have time to eat before train time. The maples is all out in full-grown leaves, 'Dory—you just ought to see 'em ! "

" Not this early, Beriah ? "

" You ought to see 'em 'Dory ; they 're like an ocean of green in the morning sunlight."

" Oh, Beriah ! "

On the train she said to him suddenly :

" I wonder why you came when you got my letter."

" Oh, shucks ! " said Beriah. " Did you think you could fool me ? How could you be run away to that Bohemia country like you said when your letter was postmarked New York as plain as day ? "

A PHILISTINE IN BOHEMIA

GEORGE WASHINGTON, with his right arm upraised, sits his iron horse at the lower corner of Union Square, for ever signalling the Broadway cars to stop as they round the curve into Fourteenth Street. But the cars buzz on, heedless, as they do at the beck of a private citizen, and the great General must feel, unless his nerves are iron, that rapid transit gloria mundi.

Should the General raise his left hand as he has raised his right, it would point to a quarter of the city that forms a haven for the oppressed and suppressed of foreign lands. In the cause of national or personal freedom they have found a refuge here, and the patriot who made it for them sits his steed, overlooking their district, while he listens through his left ear to vaudeville that caricatures the posterity of his protégés. Italy, Poland, the former Spanish possessions and the polyglot tribes of Austria-Hungary have spilled here a thick lather of their effervescent sons. In the eccentric cafés and lodging-houses of the vicinity they hover over their native wines and political secrets. The colony changes with much frequency. Faces disappear from the haunts, to be replaced by others. Whither do these uneasy birds flit?

For half of the answer observe carefully the suave foreign air and foreign courtesy of the next waiter who serves your table d'hôte. For the other half, perhaps if the barber shops had tongues (and who will dispute it?) they could tell their share.

Titles are as plentiful as finger-rings among these transitory exiles. For lack of proper exploitation, a stock of titled goods large enough to supply the trade of upper Fifth Avenue is here condemned to a mere pushcart traffic. The new-world landlords who entertain these offshoots of nobility are not dazzled by coronets and crests. They have dough-nuts to sell instead of daughters. With them it is a serious matter of trading in flour and sugar instead of pearl powder and bonbons.

These assertions are deemed fitting as an introduction to the tale, which is of plebeians, and contains no one with even the ghost of a title.

Katy Dempsey's mother kept a furnished-room house in this oasis of the aliens. The business was not profitable. If the two scraped together enough to meet the landlord's agent on rent day and negotiate for the ingredients of a daily Irish stew they called it success. Often the stew lacked both meat and potatoes. Sometimes it became as bad as consommé with music.

In this mouldy old house Katy waxed plump and pert and wholesome, and as beautiful and freckled as a tiger lily. She was the good fairy who was guilty of placing the damp clean towels and cracked pitchers of freshly-laundered Croton in the lodgers' rooms.

You are informed (by virtue of the privileges of astronomical discovery) that the star lodger's name was Mr. Brunelli. His wearing a yellow tie and paying his rent promptly distinguished him from the other lodgers. His raiment was splendid, his complexion olive, his moustache fierce, his manners a prince's, his rings and pins as magnificent as those of a travelling dentist.

He had breakfast served in his room, and he ate it in a red dressing-gown with green tassels. He left the house at noon and returned at midnight. Those were mysterious hours, but there was nothing mysterious about Mrs. Dempsey's lodgers except the things that were not mysterious. One of Mr. Kipling's poems is addressed to " Ye who hold the unwritten clue to all save all unwritten things." The same " readers " are invited to tackle the fore-going assertion.

Mr. Brunelli, being impressionable and a Latin, fell to conjugating the verb " amare," with Katy in the objective case, though not because of antipathy. She talked it over with her mother.

" Sure, I like him," said Katy. " He's more politeness than twinty candidates for Alderman, and he makes me feel like a queen whin he walks at me side. But what is he,

I dinno ?   I 've me suspicions.   The marnin 'll coom whin he 'll throt out the picture av his baronial halls and ax to have the week's rint hung up in the ice chist along wid all the rist of 'em."

" 'Tis thrue," admitted Mrs. Dempsey, " that he seems to be a sort iv a Dago, and too cool-chured in his spache for a rale gintleman.   But ye may be misjudgin' him.   Ye should niver suspect any wan of bein' of noble descint that pays cash and pathronizes the laundry rig'lar."

" He 's the same thricks of spakin' and blarneyin' wid his hands," sighed Katy, " as the Frinch nobleman at Mrs. Toole's that ran away wid Mr. Toole's Sunday pants and left the photograph of the Bastile, his grandfather's chat-taw, as security for tin weeks' rint."

Mr. Brunelli continued his calorific wooing. Katy continued to hesitate.   One day he asked her out to dine, and she felt that a dénouement was in the air.   While they are on their way, with Katy in her best muslin, you must take as an entr'acte a brief peep at New York's Bohemia.

'Tonio's restaurant is in Bohemia.   The very location of it is secret.   If you wish to know where it is ask the first person you meet. He will tell you in a whisper.   'Tonio dis-countenances custom ; he keeps his house-front black and forbidding ; he gives you a pretty had dinner ; he locks his door at the dinin bour ; but he knows spaghetti as the boardin house knows cold veal ; and—he has deposit

many dollars in a certain Banco di —— something with many gold vowels in the name on
its windows.

To this restaurant Mr. Brunelli conducted
Katy. The house was dark and the shades
were lowered ; but Mr. Brunelli touched an
electric button by the basement door, and they
were admitted.

Along a long, dark, narrow hallway they went,
and then through a shining and spotless kitchen
that opened directly upon a back yard.

The walls of houses hemmed three sides of
the yard ; a high, board fence, surrounded by
cats, the other. A wash of clothes was
suspended high upon a line stretched from
diagonal corners. Those were property clothes,
and were never taken in by 'Tonio. They were
there that wits with defective pronunciation
might make puns in connection with the
ragout.

A dozen and a half little tables set upon the
bare ground were crowded with Bohemia-
hunters, who flocked there because 'Tonio pretended not to want them and pretended to give
them a good dinner. There was a sprinkling
of real Bohemians present who came for a
change because they were tired of the real
Bohemia, and a smart shower of the men
who originate the bright sayings of Congressmen
and the little nephew of the well-known
general passenger agent of the Evansville and
Terre Haute Railroad Company.

Here is a bon mot that was manufactured at 'Tonio's :

" A dinner at 'Tonio's," said a Bohemian, " always amounts to twice the price that is asked for it."

Let us assume that an accommodating voice inquires :

" How so ? "

" The dinner costs you 40 cents ; you give 10 cents to the waiter, and it makes you feel like 30 cents."

Most of the diners were confirmed table d'hôters—gastronomic adventurers, for 'ever seeking the El Dorado of a good claret, and consistently coming to grief in California.

Mr. Brunelli escorted Katy to a little table embowered with shrubbery in tubs, and asked her to excuse him for a while.

Katy sat, enchanted by a scene so brilliant to her. The grand ladies, in splendid dresses and plumes and sparkling rings ; the fine gentle-men who laughed so loudly, the cries of " Garsong ! " and " We, monseer," and " Hello, Mame ! " that distinguish Bohemia ; the lively chatter, the cigarette smoke, the interchange of bright smiles and eye-glances—all this display and magnificence overpowered the daughter of Mrs. Dempsey and held her motionless.

Mr. Brunelli stepped into the yard, and seemed to spread his smile and bow over the entire company. And everywhere there was a great clapping of hands and a few cries o'

" Bravo ! " and " 'Tonio ! 'Tonio ! " whatever those words might mean. Ladies waved their napkins at him, gentlemen almost twisted their necks off, trying to catch his nod.

When the ovation was concluded Mr. Brunelli, with a final bow, stepped nimbly into the kitchen and flung off his coat and waistcoat.

Flaherty, the nimblest " garsong " among the waiters, had been assigned to the special service of Katy. She was a little faint from hunger, for the Irish stew on the Dempsey table had been particularly weak that day. Delicious odours from unknown dishes tantalized her. And Flaherty began to bring to her table course after course of ambrosial food that the gods might have pronounced excellent.

But even in the midst of her Lucullian repast Katy laid down her knife and fork. Her heart sank as lead, and a tear fell upon her filet mignon. Her haunting suspicions of the star lodger arose again, fourfold. Thus courted and admired and smiled upon by that fashionable and gracious assembly, what else could Mr. Brunelli be but one of those dazzling titled patricians, glorious of name but shy of rent money, concerning whom experience had made her wise ? With a sense of his ineligibility growing within her, there was mingled a torturing conviction that his personality was becoming more pleasing to her day by day. And why had he left her to dine alone ?

But here he was coming again, now coatless,

his snowy shirt-sleeves rolled high above his Jeffriesonian elbows, a white yachting cap perched upon his jetty curls.

" 'Tonio ! 'Tonio ! " shouted many, and " The spaghetti ! The spaghetti ! " shouted the rest.

Never at 'Tonio's did a waiter dare to serve a dish of spaghetti until 'Tonio came to test it, to prove the sauce, and add the needful dash of seasoning that gave it perfection.

From table to table moved 'Tonio, like a prince in his palace, greeting his guests. White, jewelled hands signalled him from every side.

A glass of wine with this one and that, smiles for all, a jest and repartee for any that might challenge—truly few princes could be so agreeable a host ! And what artist could ask for further appreciation of his handiwork ? Katy did not know that the proudest consummation of a New Yorker's ambition is to shake hands with a spaghetti chef or to receive a nod from a Broadway head waiter.

At last the company thinned, leaving but a few couples and quartet lingering over new wine and old stories. And then came Mr. Brunelli to Katy's secluded table, and drew a chair close to hers.

Katy smiled at him dreamily. She was eating the last spoonful of a raspberry roll with Burgundy sauce.

" You have seen ! " said Mr. Brunelli, laying one hand upon his collar-bone. ." I

am Antonio Brunelli ! Yes ; I am the great
'Tonio ! You have not suspect that ! I loave
you, Katy, and you shall marry with me
Is it not so ? Call me ' Antonio,' and say that
you will be mine.''

Katy's head drooped to the shoulder that
was now freed from all suspicion of having
received the knightly accolade.

"Oh, Andy," she sighed, "this is great !
Sure, I 'll marry wid ye. But why didn't
ye tell me ye was the cook ? I was near
turnin' ye down for bein' one of thim foreign
counts ! ''

FROM EACH ACCORDING TO HIS ABILITY

VUYNING left his club, cursing it softly, without any particular anger. From ten in the morning until eleven it had bored him immeasurably. Kirk with his fish story, Brooks with his Porto Rico cigars, old Morrison with his anecdote about the widow, Hepburn with his invariable luck at billiards—all these afflictions had been repeated without change of bill or scenery. Besides these morning evils Miss Allison had refused him again on the night before. But that was a chronic trouble. Five times she had laughed at his offer to make her Mrs. Vuyning. He intended to ask her again the next Wednesday evening.

Vuyning walked along Forty-fourth Street to Broadway, and then drifted down the great sluice that washes out the dust of the gold-mines of Gotham. He wore a morning suit of light grey, low, dull kid shoes, a plain, finely-woven straw hat, and his visible linen was the most delicate possible shade of helio-trope. His necktie was the blue-grey of a November sky, and its knot was plainly the outcome of a lordly carelessness, combined with an accurate conception of the most recent dictum of fashion.

223

Now, to write of a man's haberdashery is a worse thing than to write an historical novel " around " Paul Jones, or to pen a testimonial to a hay-fever cure.

Therefore, let it be known that the description of Vuyning's apparel is germane to the movements of the story, and not to make room for the new fall stock of goods.

Even Broadway that morning was a discord in Vuyning's ears ; and in his eyes it paralleled for a few dreamy, dreary minutes a certain howling, scorching, seething, malodorous slice of street that he remembered in Morocco. He saw the struggling mass of dogs, beggars, fakirs, slave-drivers, and veiled women in carts without horses, the sun blazing brightly among the bazaars, the piles of rubbish from ruined temples in the street—and then a lady, passing, jabbed the ferrule of a parasol in his side and brought him back to 'Broadway.

Five minutes of his stroll brought him to a certain corner, where a number of silent, pale-faced men are accustomed to stand, immovably, for hours, busy with the file blades of their penknives, with their hat brims on a level with their eyelids. Wall Street speculators, driving home in their carriages, love to point out these men to their visiting friends, and tell them of this rather famous lounging-place of the " crooks." On Wall Street the speculators never use the file blades of their knives.

Vuyning was delighted when one of this company stepped forth and addressed him as he was passing. He was hungry for something out of the ordinary, and to be accosted by this smooth-faced, keen-eyed, low-voiced, athetic member of the under-world, with his grim, yet pleasant smile, had all the taste of an adventure to the convention-weary Vuyning.

"Excuse me, friend," said he. "Could I have a few minutes' talk with you—on the level?"

"Certainly," said Vuyning, with a smile. "But, suppose we step aside to a quieter place. There is a divan—a café over here that will do. Schrumm will give us a private corner."

Schrumm established them under a growing palm, with two seidls between them. Vuyning made a pleasant reference to meteorological conditions, thus forming a hinge upon which might be swung the door leading from the thought repository of the other.

"In the first place," said his companion, with the air of one who presents his credentials, "I want you to understand that I am a crook. Out West I am known as Rowdy the Dude. Pickpocket, supper man, second-story man, yeggman, boxman, all-round burglar, card-sharp and slickest con man west of the Twenty-third Street ferry landing—that's my history. That's to show I'm on the square—with you My name's Emerson."

" Confound old Kirk with his fish stories,"
said Vuyning to himself, with silent glee as
he went through his pockets for a card. " It 's
pronounced ' Vining,' " he said, as he tossed
it over to the other. " And I 'll be as frank
with you. I 'm just a kind of a loafer, I guess,
living on my daddy's money. At the club
they call me ' Left-at-the-Post.' I never did
a day's work in my life ; and I haven't the
heart to run over a chicken when I 'm motoring.
It 's a pretty shabby record, altogether."

" There 's one thing you can do," said
Emerson, admiringly ; " you can carry duds.
I 've watched you several times pass on
Broadway. You look the best-dressed man
I 've seen. And I 'll bet you a gold mine
I 've got $50 worth more gent's furnishings on
my frame than you have. That 's what I
wanted to see you about. I can't do the trick.
Take a look at me. What 's wrong ? "

" Stand up," said Vuyning.

Emerson arose, and slowly revolved.

" You 've been ' outfitted,' " declared the
clubman. " Some Broadway window-dresser
has misused you. That 's an expensive suit,
though, Emerson."

" A hundred dollars," said Emerson.

" Twenty too much," said Vuyning. " Six
months old in cut, one inch too long, and half
an inch too much lapel. Your hat is plainly
dated one year ago, although there 's only a
sixteenth of an inch lacking in the brim to tell

the story. That English poke in your collar
is too short by the distance between Troy and
London. A plain gold link cuff-button would
take all the shine out of those pearl ones with
diamond settings. Those tan shoes would
be exactly the articles to work into the heart
of a Brooklyn school-ma'am on a two weeks'
visit to Lake Ronkonkoma. I think I caught
a glimpse of a blue silk sock embroidered with
russet lilies of the valley when you—improperly
—drew up your trousers as you sat down.
There are always plain ones to be had in the
stores. Have I hurt your feelings, Emerson ? "

" Double the ante ! " cried the criticised
one, greedily. " Give me more of it. There 's
a way to tote the haberdashery, and I want
to get wise to it. Say, you 're the right kind
of a swell. Anything else to the queer about
me ? "

" Your tie," said Vuyning, " is tied with
absolute precision and correctness."

" Thanks," gratefully—" I spent over half
an hour at it before I —— "

" Thereby," interrupted Vuyning, " complet-
ing your resemblance to a dummy in a
Broadway store window."

" Yours truly," said Emerson, sitting down
again. " It 's bully of you to put me wise.
I knew there was something wrong, but I
couldn't just put my finger on it. I guess it
comes by nature to know how to wear clothes."

" Oh, I suppose," said Vuyning, with a laugh,

"that my ancestors picked up the knack while they were peddling clothes from house to house a couple of hundred years ago. I'm told they did that."

"And mine," said Emerson, cheerfully, "were making their visits at night, I guess, and didn't have a chance to catch on to the correct styles."

"I tell you what," said Vuyning, whose ennui had taken wings, "I'll take you to my tailor. He'll eliminate the mark of the beast from your exterior. That is, if you care to go any farther in the way of expense."

"Play 'em to the ceiling," said Emerson, with a boyish smile of joy. "I've got a roll as big around as a barrel of black-eyed peas and as loose as the wrapper of a two-for-fiver. I don't mind telling you that I was not touring among the Antipodes when the burglar-proof safe of the Farmers' National Bank of Butter-ville, Ia., flew open some moonless nights ago to the tune of $16,000."

"Aren't you afraid," said Vuyning, "that I'll call a cop and hand you over?"

"You tell me," said Emerson, coolly, "why I didn't keep them."

He laid Vuyning's pocket-book and watch —the Vuyning 100-year-old family watch—on the table.

"Man," said Vuyning, revelling, "did you ever hear the tale Kirk tells about the six-pound trout and the old fisherman?"

" Seems not," said Emerson, politely. " I 'd like to."

" But you won't," said Vuyning. " I 've heard it scores of times. That 's why I won't tell you. I was just thinking how much better this is than a club. Now, shall we go to my tailor ? "

       *   *   *   *

" Boys, and elderly gents," said Vuyning, five days later at his club, standing up against the window where his coterie was gathered, and keeping out the breeze, " a friend of mine from the West will dine at our table this evening."

" Will he ask if we have heard the latest from Denver ? " said a member, squirming in his chair.

" Will he mention the new twenty-three-story Masonic Temple, in Quincy, Ill. ? " inquired another, dropping his nose-glasses.

" Will he spring one of those Western Mississippi River catfish stories, in which they use yearling calves for bait ? " demanded Kirk, fiercely.

" Be comforted," said Vuyning. " He has none of the little vices. He is a burglar and safe-blower, and a pal of mine."

" Oh, Mary Ann ! " said they. " Must you always adorn every statement with your alleged humour ? "

It came to pass that at eight in the evening

a calm, smooth, brilliant, affable man sat at Vuyning's right hand during dinner.   And when the ones who pass their lives in city streets spoke of sky-scrapers or of the little Czar on his far, frozen throne, or of insignificant fish from inconsequential streams, this big, deep-chested man, faultlessly clothed, and eyed like an Emperor, disposed of their Lilliputian chatter with a wink of his eyelash.

And then he painted for them with hard, broad strokes a marvellous lingual panorama of the West.   He stacked snow-topped mountains on the table, freezing the hot dishes of the waiting diners.   With a wave of his hand he swept the clubhouse into a pine-crowned gorge, turning the waiters into a grim posse, and each listener into a blood-stained fugitive, climbing with torn fingers upon the ensanguined rocks.   He touched the table and spake, and the five panted as they gazed on barren lava beds, and each man took his tongue between his teeth and felt his mouth bake at the tale of a land empty of water and food.   As simply as Homer sang, while he dug a tine of his fork leisurely into the table-cloth, he opened a new world to their view, as does one who tells a child of the Looking-Glass Country.

As one of his listeners might have spoken of tea too strong at a Madison Square " after-noon," so he depicted the ravages of " redeye " in a border town when the caballeros of the lariat and " forty-five " reduced ennui to a minimum.

And then, with a sweep of his white, unringed hands, he dismissed Melpomene, and forthwith Diana and Amaryllis footed it before the mind's eyes of the clubmen.

The savannas of the continent spread before them. The wind, humming through a hundred leagues of sage brush and mesquite, closed their ears to the city's staccato noises. He told them of camps, of ranches marooned in a sea of fragrant prairie blossoms, of gallops in the stilly night that Apollo would have forsaken his daytime steeds to enjoy ; he read them the great, rough epic of the cattle and the hills that have not been spoiled by the hand of man, the mason. His words were a telescope to the city men, whose eyes had looked upon Youngstown, O., and whose tongues had called it " West."

In fact, Emerson had them " going."

*   *   *   *   *

The next morning at ten he met Vuyning, by appointment, at a Forty-second Street café.

Emerson was to leave for the West that day. He wore a suit of dark cheviot that looked to have been draped upon him by an ancient Grecian tailor who was a few thousand years ahead of the styles.

" Mr. Vuyning," said he, with the clear, ingenuous smile of the successful " crook," " it 's up to me to go the limit for you any time

I can do so. You 're the real thing ; and if I can ever return the favour, you bet your life I 'll do it."

"What was that cow-puncher's name ? " asked Vuyning, "who used to catch a mustang by the nose and mane, and throw him till he put the bridle on ? "

"Bates," said Emerson.

"Thanks," said Vuyning. "I thought it was Yates. Oh, about that toggery business —I 'd forgotten that."

"I 've been looking for some guy to put me on the right track for years," said Emerson. "You 're the goods, duty free, and half-way to the warehouse in a red wagon."

"Bacon, toasted on a green willow switch over red coals, ought to put broiled lobsters out of business," said Vuyning. "And you say a horse at the end of a thirty-foot rope can't pull a ten-inch stake out of wet prairie ? Well, good-bye, old man, if you must be off."

At one o'clock Vuyning had luncheon with Miss Allison by previous arrangement.

For thirty minutes he babbled to her, unaccountably, of ranches, horses, cañons, cyclones, round-ups, Rocky Mountains, and beans and bacon. She looked at him with wondering and half terrified eyes.

"I was going to propose again to-day," said Vuyning, cheerily, "but I won't. I 've worried you often enough. You know dad has a ranch in Colorado. What 's the good of staying here? Jumping jonquils! but it's great out there. I'm going to start next Tuesday."

"No, you won't," said Miss Allison.

"What?" said Vuyning.

"Not alone," said Miss Allison, dropping a tear upon her salad. "What do you think?"

"Betty!" exclaimed Vuyning, "what do you mean?"

"I'll go too," said Miss Allison, forcibly.

Vuyning filled her glass with Apollinaris.

"Here's to Rowdy the Dude!" he gave— a toast mysterious.

"Don't know him," said Miss Allison; "but if he's your friend, Jimmy—here goes!"

THE MEMENTO

Miss Lynnette D'Armande turned her back on Broadway. This was but tit for tat, because Broadway had often done the same thing to Miss D'Armande. Still, the "tats" seemed to have it, for the ex-leading lady of the "Reaping the Whirlwind" Company had everything to ask of Broadway, while there was no vice versa.

So Miss Lynnette D'Armande turned the back of her chair to her window that overlooked Broadway, and sat down to stitch in time the lisle-thread heel of a black silk stocking. The tumult and glitter of the roaring Broadway beneath her window had no charm for her; what she greatly desired was the stifling air of a dressing-room on that fairyland street and the roar of an audience gathered in that capricious quarter. In the meantime, those stockings must not be neglected. Silk does wear out so, but—after all, isn't it just the only goods there is?

The Hotel Thalia looks on Broadway as Marathon looks on the sea. It stands like a gloomy cliff above the whirlpool where the tides of two great thoroughfares clash. Here the player-bands gather at the end of their wanderings, to loosen the buskin and dust the

sock. Thick in the streets around it are
booking-offices, theatres, agents, schools, and
the lobster-palaces to which those thorny
paths lead.

Wandering through the eccentric halls of the
dim and fusty Thalia, you seem to have found
yourself in some great ark or caravan about to
sail, or fly, or roll away on wheels. About the
house lingers a sense of unrest, of expectation, of
transientness, even of anxiety and apprehension.
The halls are a labyrinth. Without a guide, you
wander like a lost soul in a Sam Loyd puzzle.

Turning any corner, a dressing-sack or a
cul-de-sac may bring you up short. You meet
alarming tragedians stalking in bath-robes in
search of rumoured bathrooms. From hundreds
of rooms come the buzz of talk, scraps of new
and old songs, and the ready laughter of the
convened players.

Summer has come ; their companies have
disbanded, and they take their rest in their
favourite caravansary, while they besiege the
managers for engagements for the coming
season.

At this hour of the afternoon the day's work
of tramping the rounds of the agents' offices is
over. Past you, as you ramble distractedly
through the mossy halls, flit audible visions of
houris, with veiled, starry eyes, flying tag-ends
of things, and a swish of silk, bequeathing
to the dull hallways an odour of gaiety and
a memory of *frangipanni*. Serious young

comedians, with versatile Adam's apples, gather in doorways and talk of Booth. Far-reaching from somewhere comes the smell of ham and red cabbage, and the crash of dishes on the American plan.

The indeterminate hum of life in the Thalia is enlivened by the discreet popping—at reasonable and salubrious intervals—of beer-bottle corks. Thus punctuated, life in the genial hostel scans easily—the comma being the favourite mark, semicolons frowned upon, and periods barred.

Miss D'Armande's room was a small one. There was room for her rocker between the dresser and the wash-stand if it were placed longitudinally. On the dresser were its usual accoutrements, plus the ex-leading lady's collected souvenirs of road engagements and photographs of her dearest and best professional friends.

At one of these photographs she looked twice or thrice as she darned, and smiled friendlily.

"I'd like to know where Lee is just this minute," she said, half-aloud.

If you had been privileged to view the photograph thus flattered, you would have thought at the first glance that you saw the picture of a many-petalled white flower, blown through the air by a storm. But the floral kingdom was not responsible for that swirl of petalous whiteness.

You saw the filmy, brief skirt of Miss Rosalie Ray as she made a complete heels-over-head turn in her wistaria-entwined swing, far out from the stage, high above the heads of the audience. You saw the camera's inadequate representation of the graceful, strong kick, with which she, at this exciting moment, sent flying, high and far, the yellow silk garter that each evening spun from her agile limb and descended upon the delighted audience below.

You saw, too, amid the black-clothed, mainly masculine patrons of select vaudeville a hundred hands raised with the hope of staying the flight of the brilliant aerial token.

Forty weeks of the best circuits this act had brought Miss Rosalie Ray for each of two years. She did other things during her twelve minutes —a song and dance, imitations of two or three actors who are but imitations of themselves, and a balancing feat with a step-ladder and feather-duster ; but when the blossom-decked swing was let down from the flies, and Miss Rosalie sprang smiling into the seat, with the golden circlet conspicuous in the place whence it was soon to slide and become a soaring and coveted guerdon—then it was that the audience rose in its seat as a single man—or presumably so—and endorsed the specialty that made Miss Ray's name a favourite in the booking-offices.

At the end of the two years Miss Ray suddenly announced to her dear friend, Miss D'Armande, that she was going to spend the summer at an antediluvian village on the north shore of Long Island, and that the stage would see her no more.

Seventeen minutes after Miss Lynnette D'Armande had expressed her wish to know the whereabouts of her old chum, there were sharp raps at her door.

Doubt not that it was Rosalie Ray. At the shrill command to enter she did so, with something of a tired flutter, and dropped a heavy hand-bag on the floor. Upon my word, it was Rosalie, in a loose, travel-stained automobileless coat, closely - tied brown veil with yard-long, flying ends, grey walking-suit and tan Oxfords with lavender over-gaiters.

When she threw off her veil and hat, you saw a pretty enough face, now flushed and disturbed by some unusual emotion, and restless, large eyes with discontent marring their brightness. A heavy pile of dull auburn hair, hastily put up, was escaping in crinkly, waving strands and curling, small locks from the confining combs and pins.

The meeting of the two was not marked by the effusion vocal, gymnastical, osculatory, and catechetical that distinguishes the greetings of their unprofessional sisters in society. There was a brief clinch, two simultaneous labial dabs, and they stood on the same footing of the old days. Very much like the short salutations of soldiers or of travellers in foreign wilds are the welcomes between the strollers at the corners of their criss-cross roads.

" I 've got the hall room two flights up above yours," said Rosalie, " but I came straight to see you before going up. I didn't know you were here till they told me."

" I 've been in since the last of April," said Lynnette. " And I 'm going on the road with a ' Fatal Inheritance ' Company. We open next week in Elizabeth. I thought you 'd quit the stage, Lee. Tell me about yourself."

Rosalie settled herself with a skilful wriggle on the top of Miss D'Armande's wardrobe trunk, and leaned her head against the papered wall. From long habit, thus can peripatetic leading ladies and their sisters make themselves as comfortable as though the deepest arm-chairs embraced them.

" I 'm going to tell you, Lynn," she said, with a strangely sardonic and yet carelessly resigned look on her youthful face. " And then to-morrow I 'll strike the old Broadway trail again, and wear some more paint off the chairs in the agents' offices. If anybody had told me any time in the last three months up to four o'clock this afternoon that I 'd ever listen to that ' Leave-your-name-and-address ' rot of the booking bunch again, I 'd have given 'em the real Mrs. Fiske laugh. Loan me a handkerchief, Lynn. Gee ! but those Long Island trains are fierce. I 've got enough soft-coal cinders on my face to go on and play

Topsy without using the cork. And, speaking of corks—got anything to drink, Lynn ? "

Miss D'Armande opened a door of the washstand and took out a bottle.

" There 's nearly a pint of Manhattan. There 's a cluster of carnations in the drinking glass, but—— "

" Oh, pass the bottle. Save the glass for company. Thanks ! That hits the spot. The same to you. My first drink in three months !

" Yes, Lynn, I quit the stage at the end of last season. I quit it because I was sick of the life. And especially because my heart and soul were sick of men—of the kind of men we stage people have to be up against. You know what the game is to us—it 's a fight against 'em all the way down the line, from the manager who wants us to try his new motor-car to the bill-posters who want to call us by our front names.

" And the men we have to meet after the show are the worst of all. The stage-door kind, and the manager's friends who take us to supper, and show their diamonds, and talk about seeing 'Dan ' and ' Dave ' and ' Charlie ' for us. They 're beasts, and I hate 'em.

" I tell you, Lynn, it 's the girls like us on the stage that ought to be pitied. It 's girls from good homes that are honestly ambitious and work hard to rise in the profession, but never do get there. You hear a lot of sympathy sloshed around on chorus girls and their fifteen dollars a week. Piffle! There ain't a sorrow in the chorus that a lobster cannot heal.

"If there's any tears to shed, let 'em fall for the actress that gets a salary of from thirty to forty-five dollars a week for taking a leading part in a bum show. She knows she'll never do any better; but she hangs on for years, hoping for the 'chance' that never comes.

"And the fool plays we have to work in! Having another girl roll you around the stage by the hind legs in a 'Wheelbarrow Chorus' in a musical comedy is dignified drama compared with the idiotic things I've had to do in the thirty-centers.

"But what I hated most was the men—the men leering and blathering at you across tables, trying to buy you with Würzburger or Extra Dry, according to their estimate of your price. And the men in the audiences, clapping, yelling, snarling, crowding, writhing, gloating—like a lot of wild beasts, with their eyes fixed on you, ready to eat you up if you come in reach of their claws. Oh, how I hate 'em!

"Well, I'm not telling you much about myself, am I, Lynn?

"I had two hundred dollars saved up, and I cut the stage the first of the summer. I went over on Long Island, and found the sweetest little village that ever was, called Soundport, right on the water. I was going to spend the summer there, and study up on elocution, and try to get a class in the fall. There was an old widow lady with a cottage near the beach who sometimes rented a room or two just for company, and she took me in. She had another boarder, too—the Reverend Arthur Lyle.

"Yes, he was the head-liner. You're on, Lynn. I'll tell you all of it in a minute. It's only a one-act play.

"The first time he walked on, Lynn, I felt myself going; the first lines he spoke, he had me. He was different from the men in audiences. He was tall and slim, and you never heard him come in the room, but you *felt* him. He had a face like a picture of a knight—like one of that Round Table bunch—and a voice like a 'cello solo. And his manners!

"Lynn, if you'd take John Drew in his best drawing-room scene and compare the two, you'd have John arrested for disturbing the peace.

"I'll spare you the particulars; but in less than a month Arthur and I were engaged. He preached at a little one-night stand of a Methodist church. There was to be a parsonage the size of a lunch - wagon, and hens and honeysuckles when we were married. Arthur used to preach to me a good deal about Heaven, but he never could get my mind quite off those honeysuckles and hens.

" No ; I didn't tell him I 'd been on the stage. I hated the business and all that went with it ; I 'd cut it out for ever, and I didn't see any use of stirring things up. I was a good girl, and I didn't have anything to confess, except being an elocutionist, and that was about all the strain my conscience would stand.

" Oh, I tell you, Lynn, I was happy. I sang in the choir and attended the sewing society, and recited that ' Annie Laurie ' thing with the whistling stunt in it, ' in a manner bordering upon the professional,' as the weekly village paper reported it. And Arthur and I went rowing, and walking in the woods, and clamming, and that poky little village seemed to me the best place in the world. I 'd have been happy to live there always, too, if ——

" But one morning old Mrs. Gurley, the widow lady, got gossipy while I was helping her string beans on the back porch, and began to gush information, as folks who rent out their rooms usually do. Mr. Lyle was her idea of a saint on earth—as he was mine, too. She went over all his virtues and graces, and wound up by telling me that Arthur had had an extremely romantic love-affair, not long before, that had ended unhappily. She didn't seem to be on to the details, but she knew that he had been hit pretty hard. He was paler and thinner, she said, and he had some kind of a remembrance or keepsake of the lady in a little rosewood box that he kept locked in his desk drawer in his study.

" ' Several times,' says she, ' I 've seen him gloomerin' over that box of evenings, and he always locks it up right away if anybody comes into the room.'

" Well, you can imagine how long it was before I got Arthur by the wrist and led him down stage and hissed in his ear.

" That same afternoon we were lazying around in a boat among the water-lilies at the edge of the bay.

" ' Arthur,' says I, ' you never told me you 'd had another love-affair. But Mrs. Gurley did,' I went on, to let him know I knew. I hate to hear a man lie.

" ' Before you came,' says he, looking me frankly in the eye, ' there was a previous affection—a strong one. Since you know of it, I will be perfectly candid with you.'

" ' I am waiting,' says I.

" ' My dear Ida,' says Arthur—of course I went by my real name while I was in Soundport —' this former affection was a spiritual one, in fact. Although the lady aroused my deepest sentiments, and was, as I thought, my ideal woman, I never met her, and never spoke to her. It was an ideal love. My love for you, while no less ideal, is different. You wouldn't let that come between us.'

" ' Was she pretty ? ' I asked.

" ' She was very beautiful,' said Arthur.

" ' Did you see her often ? ' I asked.

" ' Something like a dozen times,' says he.

" ' Always from a distance ? ' says I.

" ' Always from quite a distance,' says he.

" ' And you loved her ? ' I asked.

" ' She seemed my ideal of beauty and grace —and soul,' says Arthur.

" ' And this keepsake that you keep under lock and key, and moon over at times, is that a remembrance from her ? '

" ' A memento,' says Arthur, ' that I have treasured.'

" ' Did she send it to you ? '

" ' It came to me from her,' says he.

" ' In a roundabout way ? ' I asked.

" ' Somewhat roundabout,' says he, ' and yet rather direct.'

" ' Why didn't you ever meet her ? ' I asked. ' Were your positions in life so different ? '

" ' She was far above me,' says Arthur. ' Now, Ida,' he goes on, ' this is all of the past. You 're not going to be jealous, are you ? '

" ' Jealous ! ' says I. ' Why, man, what are you talking about ? It makes me think ten times as much of you as I did before I knew about it.'

" And it did, Lynn—if you can understand it. That ideal love was a new one on me, but it struck me as being the most beautiful and glorious thing I'd ever heard of. Think of a man loving a woman he'd never even spoken to, and being faithful just to what his mind and heart pictured her Oh, it sounded great to me. The men I'd always known come at you with either diamonds, knock-out-drops or a raise of salary,—and their ideals!—well, we'll say no more.

"Yes, it made me think more of Arthur than I did before. I couldn't be jealous of that far-away divinity that he used to worship, for I was going to have him myself. And I began to look upon him as a saint on earth, just as old lady Gurley did.

"About four o'clock this afternoon a man came to the house for Arthur to go and see somebody that was sick among his church bunch. Old lady Gurley was taking her afternoon snore on a couch, so that left me pretty much alone.

"In passing by Arthur's study I looked in, and saw his bunch of keys hanging in the drawer of his desk, where he'd forgotten 'em. Well, I guess we're all to the Mrs. Bluebeard now and then, ain't we, Lynn? I made up my mind I'd have a look at that memento he kept so secret. Not that I cared what it was—it was just curiosity.

"While I was opening the drawer I imagined one or two things it might be. I thought it might be a dried rosebud she'd dropped down to him from a balcony, or maybe a picture of her he 'd cut out of a magazine, she being so high up in the world.

" I opened the drawer, and there was the rosewood casket about the size of a gent's collar box. I found the little key in the bunch that fitted it, and unlocked it and raised the lid.

" I took one look at that memento, and then I went to my room and packed my trunk. I threw a few things into my grip, gave my hair a flirt or two with a side-comb, put on my hat, and went in and gave the old lady's foot a kick. I 'd tried awfully hard to use proper and correct language while I was there for Arthur's sake, and I had the habit down pat, but it left me then.

" ' Stop sawing gourds,' says I, ' and sit up and take notice. The ghost's about to walk. I 'm going away from here, and I owe you eight dollars. The expressman will call for my trunk.'

" I handed her the money.

" ' Dear me, Miss Crosby ! ' says she. ' Is anything wrong ? I thought you were pleased here. Dear me, young women are so hard to understand, and so different from what you expect 'em to be.'

" ' You 're damn right,' says I. ' Some of 'em are. But you can't say that about men. *When you know one man you know 'em all!* That settles the human-race question.'

"And then I caught the four-thirty-eight, soft-coal unlimited ; and here I am."

"You didn't tell me what was in the box, Lee," said Miss D'Armande, anxiously.

"One of those yellow silk garters that I used to kick off my leg into the audience during that old vaudeville swing act of mine. Is there any of the cocktail left, Lynn ? "

THE END

Printed in Great Britain by J. W. Arrowsmith Ltd., Bristol.